Desolation Highway

Also by James R. Coggins

Who's Grace?

Desolation Highway

A John Smyth Mystery (#2)

JAMES R. COGGINS

MOODY PUBLISHERS
CHICAGO

All Scripture quotations, unless otherwise indicated, are taken from the Holy
Bible, New International Version®. NIV®. Copyright © 1973, 1978, 1984 by
International Bible Society. Used by permission of Zondervan Publishing
House. All rights reserved.

Library of Congress Cataloging-in-Publication Data

Coggins, James Robert, 1949-
    Desolation highway : a John Smyth mystery / James R. Coggins.
        p. cm. — (A John Smyth mystery ; #2)
    ISBN 0-8024-1766-3
    1. Periodical editors—Fiction. 2. British Columbia—Fiction.
3. Serial murders—Fiction. I. Title.

PR9199.4.C64D47 2004
813'.6--dc22

                                                            2004010477

1 3 5 7 9 10 8 6 4 2

Printed in the United States of America

For Christine and Jaeda
and the next generation
of writers and readers.

Chapter 1

WEDNESDAY, MAY 19

Mommy! I gotta go nooooow!" Sarah said for the seventeenth time.

"George, we'd better stop."

"Can't she hold it a little longer? It's only thirty-five kilometers to Prince Rupert."

The long stretch of the Yellowhead Highway follows the Skeena River through the rugged heights and dense fir forests of British Columbia's coastal mountains down to the port of Prince Rupert, halfway up Canada's Pacific coast. Long stretches of empty road wind along, uninterrupted by gas stations or rest stops. The road is traveled mostly by battered pickups and transport trucks, plus the occasional family on vacation.

"Mommy!"

"George, she's only three and a half. I think we've got to stop. If we have to, she can go into the trees."

"There's plenty of those," George agreed.

"Look over there. Stop at that truck chain-up area."

The family van rolled to a stop in the paved bulge on the other side of the highway. In midwinter, transport trucks stopped there to put chains on their tires to get them through the snow in the mountains. But this was May, late spring, with the snow melted except on the high mountains and a light misty rain hanging in the air. Sarah and her mother stepped over the guardrail and descended a few feet into the underbrush. It was because of these steps, taken on behalf of modesty, that they made the discovery.

When she had finished, Sarah announced, "Mommy, I peed on a finger."

"What? You peed on your finger?"

"No, Mommy, not *my* finger. That finger. Look."

Sergeant Troy Wesson had not taken the family's story very seriously—until Sarah's mother produced the item. It *looked* like a human finger, though the tip had been mangled or chewed somehow. It was probably worth checking out.

Sergeant Wesson was tall and athletic-looking, with black hair and a black mustache. He was a twelve-year veteran of the Royal Canadian Mounted Police, but he had no horse, just a wife and two kids. He hadn't asked to be posted to this remote corner of British Columbia, where he had served the past six years. The work was routine—long periods of patrol and paperwork punctuated by messy highway accidents and crimes of various kinds, the majority boiling down to the common factor of alcohol. Still, Prince Rupert had its compensations—affordable housing, a beautiful coastline, and a forest wilderness to hike and hunt and fish and camp in—as long as you didn't get run over by a logging truck or get lost in the desolate wilderness.

Wesson had radioed Constable Montgomery on highway

patrol to check out the chain-up area. Mrs. Mummery had given precise directions—the chain-up area on the south side of the road about thirty-five kilometers, or twenty-two miles, from town.

Within thirty minutes, Montgomery had radioed back in. He had found the spot, including the piece of ribbon Mrs. Mummery had had the presence of mind to tie to a tree branch where they entered the trees a few feet from a bear-proof garbage receptacle. However, a quick search through the bushes had revealed no other parts of a body. The chain-up area was at a place where the highway diverged from the river somewhat to run a little higher along the side of the valley. In the bush beside the chain-up area, the ground was relatively level for about six or seven feet, was sloped but manageable for another seven or eight feet, and then became much steeper, dropping away to the Skeena River Valley floor a few hundred feet below. The underbrush was thick and tangled with heavy vines. A proper search would take dogs and ropes.

Wesson told the constable to stay where he was—to secure the scene just in case. His next task was going to be a bit awkward.

Dr. Charles Haquapar was a gawky thirty-something with thinning, unkempt hair and beady brown eyes. He was one of about twenty-five doctors in Prince Rupert, and he tended to be abrupt, irritable, and somewhat lacking in bedside manner. He also coped with these problems and the isolation with regular doses of alcohol, but doctors are scarce in isolated areas, and Haquapar and the community got along fairly well. There was no official police medical examiner in Prince Rupert, but the police sometimes found that Haquapar, as a single man with a mediocre practice, was more readily available to give medical opinions in police cases than other local doctors. Wesson found Haquapar at the small hospital that served Prince Rupert and the surrounding area.

"Okay, you called for a medical examiner. Where's the body?"

"Here." Wesson carefully held out the finger in a plastic bag.

"A finger? It's going to be hard to make an identification or fixed cause of death from this. What do you want me to do with it?"

"First, tell me if it's genuine. Is it a real finger?"

After a short examination, Haquapar looked up. "Yes. It appears to be a genuine human finger, all right."

"How old is it?"

"It's tough to tell the age of a patient from a finger."

"I mean how long since it was separated from its hand?"

"Hard to say. At least a week, probably quite a bit longer. Where's the rest of the body?"

"I don't know. It could be walking around somewhere. This was found at a truck chain-up area about thirty-five clicks out." Wesson did not have to specify the road. There was only one highway in and out of Prince Rupert, a forestry town, fishing village, port, and service center for a number of local Native reserves.

"A chain-up area?"

"Yeah. Have you treated anyone for a missing finger lately?"

"You think maybe a trucker lost a finger in a chain or something?"

"Maybe."

"No. Nothing like that. Maybe one of the other doctors has. Or maybe he was going the other way."

"Well, it was on the south side of the road, but it is accessible to traffic going either way. We'll check with Terrace and Prince George."

Haquapar shrugged.

"But you accept that it could be a trucker?"

"Could be, but it's not a large finger."

"But it did belong to a man?"

"Not necessarily. Fingers don't have sex organs. It could be a woman or a medium- to small-sized man. It doesn't rule out your theory though—there are women truckers now. DNA testing could tell you, but we can't do that here."

"Can you tell how it was separated from the hand?"

"I'm not an expert on such things, but it is a somewhat ragged cut. It could have been pinched and torn off by a chain or, more likely, cut off with a saw."

"Could it have come from a logger, cut off by a chainsaw?"

"Sure. That's another possibility. A knife would have left a clean edge. The tip of the finger looks like it was mangled in the same way, but perhaps it was chewed by an animal after it was cut off."

Wesson arranged for inquiries to be made in Terrace and Prince George regarding a trucker or logger with a missing finger. Terrace was the next town of any size farther up the highway, and Prince George was a larger center where the Yellowhead Highway intersected with another highway about seven hundred kilometers east of Prince Rupert. Wesson called in a dog team and a rock-climbing team for the next morning, as well as a crime-scene forensics team from Prince George. He also insisted that a patrol car remain at or near the chain-up area all night to protect the scene from interference, although that did not seem very likely at this point.

Chapter 2

THURSDAY, MAY 20

The prairie city of Winnipeg, Manitoba, lies two thousand kilometers to the east of Prince Rupert, just beyond the other end of the Yellowhead Highway. An aging, laid-back city located where two broad prairie rivers merge, the city boasts a challenging climate, a rich history, and—in the springtime at least—an array of potholes to challenge the most intrepid of drivers.

The driver of this particular taxi fit that description, John Smyth reflected as his cab jolted along the familiar route toward the airport. A short, dumpy man with wire-rimmed glasses, a red beard, and a bald head, Smyth leaned back against the cracked vinyl seat, his thoughts a jumble of ideas as random as the placement of the potholes. The taxi moved rapidly down a street lined with gnarled old elm trees, weaving around cars parked sporadically at the curb. Behind the cars and the trees were rundown houses, many of them tiny, one-bedroom structures. Even the larger one-and-a-half-story homes showed peeling paint and dingy stucco. The gaudy purple or bright yellow paint on a few of them indicated they had at some point been owned by a Ukrainian family.

This was North Winnipeg, Winnipeg north of the railroad tracks. Many of these houses, Smyth knew, were a century old, and this had been a poor area even when they were built. In those days Winnipeg had been hailed as the gateway to Canada's West, and a great tidal wave of humanity had flooded through the region. They were European castoffs, many of them—Ukrainians, Russians, Jews, Mennonites, and Poles. They had come seeking free land of their own and an opportunity to build a future, and many had eventually found those things, but at first they'd found a hard climate and an even harder life. Many had made their first Canadian homes in these tiny houses north of the tracks. Crowded several families together in a single house, they had struggled to survive, many of them succumbing to poverty, hunger, and disease.

This was historic territory. It was here in these squalid neighborhoods that Reverend J. S. Woodsworth and others had founded the Canadian socialist party, which still existed. Smyth would not say that he was a socialist himself, but he admired the compassion that had driven those early socialists, many of them Christian ministers and other proponents of the social gospel. They had been motivated not by some abstract ideology but by a passionate concern for the suffering poor.

This, too, was the area where the Grace Evangelical Church had had its beginnings, through a revival that responded to spiritual as well as economic poverty. Unlike the early socialists, the founders of the denomination had managed that rare feat of balancing compassion for the poor with a passion for orthodox Christian theology. While the party of J. S. Woodsworth had evolved into a secular socialism, Grace

Evangelical Church had retained its Christian identity. Smyth had even more sympathy for that viewpoint. He was, after all, editor of *Grace* magazine, the official publication of the five hundred Grace Evangelical churches now spread across North America.

Many of those early immigrants had moved on—to prosperous farms and elegant suburbs in Manitoba and the provinces of Saskatchewan, Alberta, and British Columbia farther to the west—but Grace Evangelical Church had kept its international headquarters here in inner-city Winnipeg. The original immigrants had been replaced by other inhabitants, equally poor and often more hopeless—displaced Natives from northern Manitoba reserves as well as more recent immigrants from Vietnam, India, the Philippines, and Latin America.

Smyth, a third-generation Winnipegger of immigrant stock, had stayed here too. He found that his church salary stretched a little further when he and his family lived in an older house in one of the better inner-city neighborhoods, and he liked living within walking distance of his office in the denominational headquarters.

The large bridge the taxi was bumping over now spanned not a river but a set of railroad tracks—the same Canadian Pacific Railway tracks that had brought the first waves of immigrants to the Canadian prairies. Farther to the south, hiding behind the purifying bulwark of the Assiniboine River, were the houses of the wealthier citizens. But here, squeezed between the railroad and the river, lay rail yards and factories, warehouses and slaughterhouses. From here the grain of the western prairies was shipped to the hungry stomachs of eastern Canada and Europe. From here beef cattle were also shipped or slaughtered to fill more empty stomachs. Here factories had sprung up to produce goods for the prairie farmers, struggling to compete with bigger, better-equipped factories in the east.

To his right, Smyth saw the massive stone towers that dominated this area of Winnipeg by sheer bulk—an ugly gray landmark. They were the buildings of the old Winnipeg Cold Storage. It had always seemed strange to Smyth that such a massive structure was needed to keep things cold in Winnipeg, a city that every year struggled through six months of a winter more extreme than that of almost any other large city on earth.

But spring was here now, and Smyth was glad of it—even though, from his viewpoint high over the tracks, there was scant evidence of it in the bleak industrial district and the tangle of railroad tracks. And he was looking forward to his trip west. Or trips west. There was the convention this weekend in Calgary, Alberta, near the western edge of the prairies. Then, in another week or so, he would head west again, to the coast of British Columbia, to visit a church in a port town called Prince Rupert.

The RCMP search team found the second finger about nine forty that morning.

Sergeant Wesson had been at the chain-up area outside Prince Rupert since about seven thirty, but the search teams and dogs from Prince George hadn't arrived until after eight. They'd begun with a sweep all along the edge of the chain-up area, tramping back and forth and, with each pass, working their way down the slope. They moved slowly, searching between and beneath the abundant undergrowth. When they finally discovered a second finger nestled up against a tree, the digit was carefully photographed and cataloged before being moved.

Around ten forty, the dogs sniffed out yet another finger about seven feet down into the bush, evidently not far from where the first one had lain. Like the first two, it appeared to have been mangled somehow at the tip.

Was this some kind of practical joke? Wesson wondered fleetingly. *Human fingers scattered throughout the bush?*

It was another half hour before they found an arm. At that point they knew, if they had not before, that the matter was serious.

John Smyth's taxi arrived at the airport an hour before his flight, in plenty of time for boarding at a small city airport like Winnipeg's. He stowed his battered briefcase in the overhead compartment, settled into his seat, and pulled out a dog-eared bundle of proofreading to work on.

A few moments later, the plane rolled down the runway, lurched, and hopped into the sky. It rose up through a heavy drizzle and was soon engulfed in thick, black clouds. As it circled and turned, searching out its flight path to Calgary, twelve hundred kilometers to the west, Smyth looked somewhat apprehensively out the window. The previous summer, looking out the window of another plane, he had witnessed a murder. This time, however, the rain and cloud obscured his view. He could see nothing on the ground below, and that was just as well.

Being involved with a murder investigation had been interesting. But as far as John Smyth was concerned, once in a lifetime was quite enough.

Sporadic traffic whirred by the chain-up area outside Prince Rupert. One or two cars stopped in briefly but were quickly waved on by the police as the search continued. It was getting on toward noon when Wesson heard one of the searchers call up to the paved area, "Sergeant, I think you might want to see this for yourself."

He clambered down through the brush. There, rolled against a tree, was a human head. The long blonde hair indicated it was probably female, but the head was too disfigured to tell anything more.

"It's like someone took a chainsaw to her face," said Corporal Len Archbold in a repressed voice, his sandy mustache twitching.

Wesson nodded grimly. *A chainsaw murderer in real life? In Canada?* The whole scenario seemed slightly unreal.

"Get the photos and take it on up," he said.

By midafternoon, they had searched the level ground and the manageable slope and then sent the teams on ropes another five or ten feet down the steeper slope toward the bottom of the valley. In that time, Wesson figured they had recovered about all they were likely to find—the head, the female torso, two legs, two arms, and seven fingers, all mangled at the tips.

The body parts were packed in ice and taken to Prince Rupert for the flight to the RCMP lab in Vancouver, the largest city in the province, about eight hundred fifty kilometers farther south. This situation clearly required a level of expertise greater than Charles Haquapar—or any medical professional in Prince Rupert—possessed.

Chapter 3

FRIDAY, MAY 21

Wesson had barely arrived at the police station the next morning when the phone rang. He picked up the receiver from the corner of the neat desk in the orderly cubicle that served as a private office for the head of the Prince Rupert RCMP detachment. On the other end of the line was Dr. Decoran from the lab in Vancouver.

"Already? I didn't expect to hear from you for hours yet," Wesson said. "You can't have completed your examination already. What did you do, stay up all night?"

"No. We've barely begun, but there was something very obvious that we wanted to ask you about."

"Sure. What?"

"Are you sure you searched the area thoroughly?"

"Yeah, pretty thoroughly. I know the body's short a couple of fingers, but other than that . . ."

"That's not quite what's worrying us."

"What is?"

"The body has two left thumbs."

"What?!"

"The body has two left—"

"Yeah, yeah, I heard you," Wesson interrupted. "Are you sure? I mean, I guess you know your business, but is that possible?"

"That's not all. One arm is longer than the other."

A mix-and-match body? Wesson's mind was whirling. *This was like a bad Frankenstein movie. Then the light began to dawn.*

"The point is," Decoran was saying, "one of the arms and at least one thumb don't come from this body. Are you sure you searched the area sufficiently?"

Evidently not. The case was getting more bizarre. A *serial* chainsaw murderer?

Wesson's next phone call was from a reporter for a Vancouver television station. *It figures,* Wesson thought. *Every horror movie needs an audience.*

Remarkably, the first day's search had attracted no media attention. The Mummery family had evidently kept quiet about their gruesome discovery, and the search teams had had little time to talk. There were some advantages to working in an isolated area.

I'll have to get someone to issue a statement, Wesson thought frantically.

"Sergeant, are you there?" the reporter's voice demanded.

"Yes, I can confirm that we have found a body. We don't yet know the identity of the victim or the cause of death." (How could he say *chainsaw?*) "We will issue a more detailed statement later today."

"But—" the voice began.

Wesson hung up.

Fortunately, the search team had decided to spend the night in Prince Rupert rather than drive all the way back to Prince George the evening before. This time, they extended the search deeper into the valley, examining the steep slope all the way down to the bottom. This time the search was watched from a distance by three reporters and a cameraman who had arrived during the morning and were kept at one end of the chain-up area.

At midmorning the searchers sent up another find, this time a man's torso, partly devoured by animals. The searchers also found another head with the face disfigured, an arm, two legs, and four more fingers, one lodged in the fork of a tree. Late in the day they called off the search, and the new body parts were duly shipped off to Vancouver.

Wesson glanced over at the reporters. For the last few hours, they had been sitting in or leaning on their vehicles at the far end of the chain-up area, occasionally talking on satellite phones or conversing with each other. When the search teams began to pack up, the reporters had suddenly become alert. Wesson recognized Skip Jackson, a pimply faced twenty-two-year-old junior reporter for the *Prince Rupert Gazette*—evidently sent out on his first major assignment by editor Marge Oldham. He also recognized a television reporter from a Vancouver television station, although he couldn't remember her name. The third reporter he didn't recognize.

Wesson walked over. "Good evening. I am Sergeant Wesson from Prince Rupert RCMP," he said. "Who are you?"

The question was addressed to the unknown third reporter, who identified himself as Jason Thuringer, a stringer for a Vancouver newspaper.

"What's going on, Sergeant?" The television reporter asked the first question.

"We have found two bodies in this location. The identities of the victims are not yet known. We do not know the cause of death, but the deaths are suspicious, and the bodies appear to have been here for some time."

"What can you tell us about the victims? Are they male, female?" The other reporters seemed content to let the television reporter ask the questions. They seemed a little intimidated by her status.

"One was a man and the other a woman, but we are not releasing any further information at this time."

"Sergeant, what were you bringing up in the black plastic bags? Why didn't we see a full body being carried up? Were the bodies dismembered?" It was the question they had all been waiting for, and it brought the conversation to a halt.

After a pause, Wesson replied, "The bodies had been here some time and were somewhat disintegrated. We don't know how."

The reporter, sensing a major story, went in for the kill: "Were the bodies cut up? Are we talking about a serial killer here, a Jack the Ripper or Jeffrey Dahmer?"

Wesson was frozen for an instant, staring into the eye of the camera. "It is far too early to reach any conclusions," he said at last. "We just don't know." He waved his hand in a futile gesture. "We may be able to tell you more . . ." Leaving the sentence trailing, he walked back to his car.

When he walked back into the police station, a tired Wesson immediately caught a wary but relieved expression on the dark, intriguing face of Mildred Stone Mountain, the dispatcher. "Inspector Travis is on line two," she said.

Wesson suddenly felt more alert. He went into the private

office and shut the door. Inspector Travis was the head of the Prince Rupert RCMP detachment, temporarily away in Vancouver to work on an administrative reorganization task force. He had left Wesson in charge.

Picking up the phone, Wesson stated crisply, "Inspector Travis, this is Sergeant Wesson."

"Wesson, it's about these bodies," the voice at the other end of the line barked. "What's the latest?"

"We have found other parts of a second body, this time a male, cut up and mangled like the other. They're on the way down to Vancouver now."

"Have you made an identification yet?"

"No. There was no ID on the bodies, of course."

"I know that, but have you matched the bodies to any missing persons?"

"No, sir, not yet."

"Have you tried?"

"Just the basics, sir. As you know, there are no active missing persons files here, and we were waiting for the lab to tell us something about the bodies—they were kind of hard to identify, to know what we're looking for. I mean, one's a woman and one's a man, but other than that, we don't know much."

"Don't give me excuses. Get on it. You've already messed up this investigation once by missing the second body. Don't mess up again. If you do, I'll put someone in charge who knows what investigation is."

"I don't think there's any need for that, sir," Wesson said. "It seems a fairly straightforward investigation from here on—"

"All right. I'll leave it for now, but I want to see some results pretty quick."

There was a sharp click. Wesson started to replace the now-silent receiver, then put it back to his ear and dialed his wife. It was starting to look like the beginning of a long evening.

Sitting at the desk, Wesson spent the rest of the evening marshaling his meager resources. Responsible for an area of hundreds of square kilometers, his RCMP detachment had only thirty officers, and a murder investigation would mean hours of overtime for them all. Saturday was Wesson's day off, but he decided to call a staff meeting for eight the next morning. He assigned two of the most senior officers, Corporal Archbold and Constable Pierre Leblanc, who had shifts scheduled that evening, to do some preliminary paperwork. Leblanc could check through the missing-persons files. And Archbold could check whether there was anyone living near the chain-up area and who thus might be a witness or a suspect.

Chapter 4

SATURDAY, MAY 22

Saturday morning, Sergeant Wesson presided over an uncustomary staff meeting. "For the next few weeks," he said, "this murder case is going to take a lot of our time. Archbold, Leblanc, Johnson, Rumple, Simmons, and I will work on the murders while the rest of you take care of the routine patrols and our other work. But all of you at all times are to be thinking about this case and looking for evidence. Every time you stop someone for speeding or pick up a drunk, see it as an opportunity to look for links to the murders. Got that?" Given the informal manner in which the detachment had become accustomed to operate in the absence of Inspector Travis, the unusual situation inevitably had had a disorienting effect. Wesson, unfortunately, had assumed a manner that seemed pompous even to himself.

The other officers nodded, fully aware of how pretentious the sergeant was sounding. Yet most of them welcomed the opportunity to work on a significant case. Besides providing a welcome break from drunk drivers, petty thefts, and domestic disputes, it offered them an opportunity to test and extend their abilities, perhaps even attract the attention of the regional commanders and earn a promotion.

"Leblanc," Wesson continued, "what did you find in our missing-persons files?"

"Officially . . ." Pierre Leblanc paused. This wasn't Vancouver, after all. Every one of the officers present could probably have recited the official list of missing persons from memory. "Officially," he repeated, "there have been four people reported missing along the Yellowhead Highway in the past year, most of these cases not originating in our jurisdiction. John Anderson and Abraham Rempel, two hunters from Vancouver, disappeared in November. We think they might have gone into the woods closer to the Prince George end of the highway, but their truck—a pickup with a canopy on the back—was found, stripped, near the Nootkasin Indian Reserve—"

"Native reserve." Wesson, as a senior officer in a "sensitive area," had completed a minority awareness course. He made the correction automatically.

"What?" Leblanc paused. "Oh . . . anyway, a large search was mounted. Nothing was ever found of either man. Can't read much into that. They were north of the highway. There are thousands of kilometers of mountain and forest out there to get lost in. If they got lost, they could still be walking."

"More likely froze to death last winter," Len Archbold put in, "or got eaten by a grizzly, or fell off a cliff."

"Either way, if anybody finds them out there now, it will be sheer luck. Of course, we're not even sure they're out there. They weren't reported missing for over two weeks after we think they went into the woods. Seems Rempel's business had gone belly-up and he was a widower—no kids. Anderson was unemployed and in the middle of a nasty divorce. Both were in their late fifties. Nobody seems to have cared much that they were gone. They wouldn't have been reported as soon as they were if Rempel hadn't been expected at some relative's birthday party out on the prairies somewhere. When he didn't show up, the birthday boy started checking. It was about that time we found the truck, which wasn't very valuable anyway. Speculation was they might have used the opportunity to leave their problems behind and go off and start over someplace where nobody knew them. Or they might have made a suicide pact and shot each other. Or one of them might have been despondent enough to shoot the other and himself. Or they might have quarreled and one shot the other and then just beat it out of there, or shot himself in remorse. Or—"

"Okay, we get the idea," Wesson interrupted. "Just about anything's possible. What about the truck?"

"We never found out anything definite on that. No fingerprints. No parts turned up. However, we picked up a rumor that an Indian—uh, Native—from Nootkasin was hitchhiking back from Prince George and found the truck abandoned, so he 'borrowed' it to drive back to the reserve, then ditched it, taking a few spare parts. That was supposedly two weeks after the hunters were last seen and just before the search began. Of course, the truck was pushed into the bush near the Nootkasin Reserve, so we can't be sure how long it was sitting there either. We didn't find it until four or five days after the search began."

"Nobody else had noticed the truck in the two weeks it had been sitting beside the road waiting for this Native fellow to come along?" Archbold asked incredulously.

"Rumor was that it was down an old logging road, and the Native found it when he hiked up the road to relieve himself."

"That was one lucky Native," Archbold said with a smirk.

"And the 'rumor,' if I recall, came from Bear Miniwac, chief of the Nootkasin band council?" Wesson said.

"Presumably. When it began to appear that something bad might have happened to the hunters—other than having their truck stolen, of course—Mr. Miniwac reported a rumor that was circulating among his people. The rumor was apparently quite detailed—definite about the truck being taken two weeks after the hunters disappeared, for instance. But despite his best efforts, the chief was unable to determine the source of the rumor."

"And we were as well?" Wesson asked.

"If the chief could not track down the rumor among his own people, it is unlikely that outsiders such as ourselves would get very far."

"Some suspicion fell upon Bear's son Daniel, I think," put in Archbold.

"Suspicion has a way of doing that to Daniel and his friends quite frequently. But Bear was sure that, whoever the rumor came from, it certainly couldn't have involved Daniel, who was safe at home that week with a sprained knee. No medical evidence, of course."

"It could be obtained. I'm sure the Native healing man could recall attending the injured boy," Wesson pointed out. "He probably wouldn't have gone to the white medical clinic."

"I might prefer the Native healer myself," Lynn Johnson suggested. "I wouldn't be that anxious to have, say, Dr. Haquapar work on me."

"Haquapar's okay—when he's sober," advised Archbold with a hint of a smile.

Johnson ignored Archbold. "Speaking of Haquapar," she asked Wesson, "when is the autopsy report due?"

"Supposed to be here sometime today," Wesson replied. "But that brings us back to the point. Could one of our bodies be a hunter from Vancouver?"

"Or both?" Johnson asked.

"No," Wesson answered. "One of the bodies was female."

"One of the hunters could have been in the truck when it was borrowed," Leblanc speculated.

"Then why would the Native drive most of the way down the highway before dumping the body at the chain-up area?" asked Wesson.

"Maybe he didn't know he was there. Maybe the hunter was in the back under the canopy—asleep or injured or even dead. If the truck was moving, maybe the chain-up area was the first opportunity the hunter had to get out and confront Daniel."

"So Daniel, or whoever the thief was, killed the hunter at the chain-up area, cut up the body, and threw it over the bank?" Wesson asked. "Maybe. But who is the other body—the woman?"

"Yes, not likely that two different murderers at different times just happened to murder and chop up a body there."

"Perhaps one of the hunters had a girlfriend," Johnson suggested.

"Then what happened to the other hunter?" Leblanc parried.

"No." Wesson held up a hand. "We're not calling the dogs out again. We would have found some trace if there was a third body there."

"Perhaps somewhere else?" Archbold suggested.

"In any case, no fresh blood was found in the truck," Leblanc continued. "And that's about all we have learned about the hunters."

"Get onto Vancouver and see if the hunters have ever turned up or if they are still missing," Wesson directed.

Leblanc made a note.

"Who else is in our missing-persons files?" Wesson prompted.

"Gracie Levasseur," Leblanc said. "Age twenty-three. We were contacted by her family in Ontario late last fall. They

29

had received a letter from her postmarked Prince Rupert. Evidently they hadn't heard from her for months before that. In the letter, she made some vague comments about finding a real family, so they guessed she might have joined some kind of commune out here. Or maybe she just found a man—the reference was quite vague."

"We visited the Lights' place, I think," Wesson said.

"Oh yes. Evidently a woman fitting Gracie's general description had been living there through the fall. They called her 'Shine.' But the description they could give of her was pretty general."

"They couldn't shed much light on the case?" Archbold asked.

"It is surprising Ray and Sun remembered her at all. She had been gone at least a couple of weeks by then."

"They'd been eating too many magic mushrooms in the interval," Archbold suggested.

"Precisely. Or perhaps they just prefer to keep things simple. Plus, Ray and Sun have so many young women passing through out there that they probably start to blur together after a while. I never have figured out how Ray manages to attract so many. Every stray waif who passes through here seems to end up there."

Archbold rolled his eyes. "Ray is a beacon of light in the wilderness."

"Yeah, but he doesn't seem to be able to hold them for long. They find out pretty quick how he wants to enlighten them, and then they take off. Or Ray gets tired of them pretty quick, or maybe Sun gets jealous—we've never been able to figure out just what goes on."

"Ray isn't even a success as a cult leader," Archbold said.

"No. Can't compete with the real weirdos."

"Did we ever figure out what Ray's and Sun's real names are?" Johnson asked.

"No. They don't collect welfare, and we don't know how they earn enough money to live on," Leblanc answered. "According to our file on them, their place was thoroughly searched a few times ten or fifteen years ago, but either they had no personal papers or they had hidden them very well. We never found anything against them, so we didn't put too much energy into investigating."

"What about Gracie Levasseur?" Wesson asked.

"As I said, the woman who fit her description had been gone at least a couple of weeks. That was confirmed by a couple of other temporary guests." He consulted his notes for the names. "Moon, a.k.a. Luther Malone, a thirty-one-year-old male from California, and Lucid, a.k.a. Amber Long, from Alberta. Amber Long definitely was not Gracie Levasseur, by the way. Amber was short and dark, Gracie about five foot seven and blonde. We searched Ray and Sun's place, even walked around in the woods in the area, but we found no trace of Gracie Levasseur. Ray and Sun weren't acting suspicious, at least no more suspicious than usual. No one had seen Gracie in Prince Rupert, so we just assumed she had hitchhiked back out to Prince George."

"So that's all we know about Gracie Levasseur?" Wesson asked.

"Yup."

"Get in touch with the Levasseur family and see if Gracie has turned up anywhere else."

Leblanc made another note.

"Who's the fourth missing person?" Archbold asked.

"A twenty-two-year-old girl from the Nootkasin Reserve."

"There has to be more than one Native girl who's run off." Archbold snorted. "There must be dozens, most of them living on the streets in Vancouver."

"True. However, only one has been officially reported

missing to the police—Kathy Miniwac, the chief's daughter. We know she was in Vancouver in October, but some people who knew her there said she was planning to hitchhike home. She never showed up here, so in November Bear reported her missing. Some inquiries were made, but police couldn't find anyone who remembered seeing her hitchhiking."

"A Native girl hitchhiking wouldn't attract much attention," Archbold suggested.

"Precisely."

"And no one who had picked her up would be eager to come forward and tell the police."

"Yes. The case is still officially open, although not under active investigation."

"Maybe I should check with the chief for an update," Wesson said, "but our Jane Doe was obviously not a Native. So . . . that's it?" He started to rise.

"Sort of."

"Sort of?"

"There is one other possibility. Anne Morrison."

"Morrison?" Wesson scratched his head. "As in Ron and Anne Morrison?"

"Yup. Couple from Winnipeg. Came out on their honeymoon last summer, camped in the park about a hundred kilometers east of here. Went canoeing on the river, hit a rock or a log. Ron made it to shore, and Anne was last seen going under in the middle of the river. River was running pretty high about then. Her body was never found."

"So what do you think?" Archbold asked. "She escaped from the river only to be murdered later?"

"Was the drowning an accident? Did anyone ask whether her husband might have killed her on purpose?" Lynn Johnson asked quietly. New to the detachment, she had not been in the area the previous summer.

"We always suspect the husband," Wesson replied firmly. "In this case, the incident took place near the campground and was witnessed by half a dozen campers. The Morrisons' canoe was caught in the current, neither was experienced in canoeing, and both appeared to be trying frantically to paddle the canoe to safety. They were shouting, and that attracted attention. When the canoe struck the rock, it spun around. The husband landed in the water near some rocks and snagged logs; the wife was flung out into the current." Wesson paused. "It's true we never recovered the body, but the guess is it reached the ocean long ago. Not likely it would be found in pieces high up on the side of the valley."

Johnson nodded.

"That's it?" Wesson asked.

"Yes," Leblanc replied. "We have photos of the missing people, of course." He began passing around some eight-by-ten glossies.

There was a pause as the officers looked at the pictures and considered Leblanc's report.

"Quite a range of people," Johnson observed.

"No kidding." Archbold chortled. "Look at the nose on this one."

"Okay," Wesson cut in. "Some possibles, but there's not a lot there. As far as I can see, none of these stand out as likely identities for the bodies we found. Anything occur to anyone else?"

The other officers shrugged and murmured agreement.

"The problem," Archbold said, "is that a lot of people up here are loners. Many of them could go missing and no one would ever know—or care."

Johnson looked around at the others. "I always thought there was a greater sense of community in small towns, that people cared for each other more."

"Is that really what you have experienced here?" Wesson

asked. "Sure, there is a sense of community, and people do take care of each other, but there is also something about the mountains and the forests that attracts people who want to get lost. This isn't just Vancouver with fewer people. When I was transferred here, another officer told me that most people in places like this are running away from something. I thought he was kidding, but the longer I've been here, the more I'm convinced he was right. We have plenty of good, stable people here, but there are also a lot of people running away from things—criminal charges, debts, alimony and child support, bad marriages, broken relationships, family expectations, the rat race, stressful jobs, moral restrictions, traditional religion, conventional social expectations. The mountains and forests are good places to hide. When you come here, you can get away from everybody and everything you've known and be and do anything you want."

There was a long silence. The officers looked as if they had just been lectured. Some appeared to be pondering if the words might be true. Finally, Wesson turned to Archbold. "Archie, what do we know about anyone living in the vicinity of the chain-up area?"

Archbold had been posted in Prince Rupert longer than the others, including Wesson, so the sergeant had assigned him responsibility for checking out the local angle. He opened a file. "I've checked the municipal records," he said. "Officially, there are three residences within a couple of kilometers either way."

"Officially?" Lynn Johnson asked.

"There's a lot of wilderness out there, and we pretty much stick to the roads. This area is perfect for hermits, loners, prospectors, renegade In—uh, Natives—living off the reserve. Any one of them—or hundreds of 'em—could walk a few hundred yards off the road, build a cabin or a lean-to, and no one

34

would ever know if they didn't want anyone to. It's not worth tramping through thousands of hectares of bush just to charge property tax on a cabin that cost five hundred dollars to build. The municipality doesn't even try to keep perfect records."

"Who are the official residents?" Wesson broke in.

"The closest is Gerard Hawkins. In fact, I think his place overlooks the chain-up area."

"Hawkins? I don't think I know him," Wesson said.

"I don't think I do either, but the name sounds familiar."

"Who else lives up there?"

"Mary Pendragon has a place about a kilometer west of the chain-up area."

"Pendragon?" Lynn Johnson said. "Doesn't anyone around here have a normal name?"

"The third residence is owned by Gary and Heather Thompson."

"Do you know anything about these people?" Wesson asked.

"Not much. The Pendragon woman's been there for a long time. The Thompsons bought their place a couple of years ago."

"I'll go out and check them all today," Wesson said. "We'll have another meeting of the six of us on the task force tonight at eight."

The bear was magnificent, with a finely chiseled head and fierce, glaring eyes. Standing motionless, it dominated the work space under a huge tarpaulin canopy that covered a clearing in front of the cabin. The cabin itself was a compact, well-proportioned log structure.

Wesson turned back to the finely chiseled figure. Standing on an as yet unformed log, it held something in its mouth, a salmon perhaps—a magnificent grizzly emerging out of the wood. Around it were a half-dozen other carved wooden figures in various stages of completion.

"You want something?"

For a moment, Wesson had the impression that the bear had spoken. But the voice came from a tall man with jet-black hair, a black beard, and a long, sharp nose. Wearing blue jeans and a red plaid lumberman's shirt, he had just walked around the corner of the cabin with a chainsaw in his hand.

"Are you Gerard Hawkins?" Wesson asked.

The big man nodded as he walked toward Wesson.

"I'm Sergeant Wesson of the RCMP. I want to ask you a few questions." When Hawkins did not respond, Wesson continued. "From this clearing, you can see the highway and the chain-up area. Have you noticed anything unusual down there?"

Hawkins, about ten feet from Wesson now, turned and looked down toward the highway a couple of thousand feet below him. The cabin, screened by the trees, was invisible from the road, but parts of the clearing allowed an unobstructed view. "Yes," he said.

"What?"

"Bunch of police cars, a couple of days ago."

"I mean earlier, say in the last couple of months?"

"Nope. Nothing comes to mind."

"We found two bodies in the bush below the chain-up area," Wesson explained, "a man and a blonde woman. We think they had been there awhile. Have you ever seen anybody like that?"

"A man and a blonde woman? Never seen anyone in my whole life like that." Only narrowed eyes and a twitch of the lips hinted the man was being sarcastic, and the flicker of amusement was instantly gone. "You got pictures? What were they wearing?"

"No, we don't have pictures yet. And they weren't wearing anything." Wesson paused a moment, glancing at the chainsaw, pondering how much he should reveal. "The bodies were cut up. We found them in pieces. Did you see or hear any-thing that could have been a murder—a gunshot, a chainsaw, people fighting in the chain-up area, anybody dumping some-thing heavy in the bush?"

Hawkins pondered this a moment. "Nope."

"Could you have seen either of the victims separately, a man or a blonde woman?"

"You seen my driveway. It's a kilometer or so up through the woods. I don't get many people droppin' in."

"Thank you, Mr. Hawk—" Wesson stopped. He pointed to the carved bear and other figures. "Is this your work?"

Hawkins nodded.

"You're the guy who does chainsaw carvings of bears and eagles and things under the name *Hawk?*"

Again Hawkins nodded.

Wesson looked around at the wooden figures. Besides the salmon-eating bear on a log, the clearing held a couple of eagles, a pair of bear cubs climbing a tree trunk, a roughly carved log that could have been a small bear standing on its hind legs, a hunter holding a gun, and a couple of other pieces that the carving had not yet advanced enough to identify. A number of bare logs were stacked at the back edge of the canopy. "They're very good," Wesson said.

Turning toward his car, he pulled a card from his pocket. "If you think of anything that might relate to the bodies we found, please let me know."

Again Hawkins just nodded.

Driving slowly down the long driveway, Wesson pondered why he had chosen to talk to Hawkins first. *The sculptor's place was closest to the chain-up area,* he told himself. But he knew there was more to it than that. Serial killers were usually men —lone men.

Back at the highway, he turned east and drove a half kilometer to where a small bungalow, more suited to a subdivision than this wilderness, sat incongruously in a good-sized clearing higher up the slope and a couple of hundred yards off the road. A few yards up the drive, he had to get out of the car to open and then reclose a chain-link gate that blocked the way. Pulling into the clearing, he noticed a logging truck at the side nearest the driveway and a doorless machine shed with implements lining the walls. Wesson noted a couple of chainsaws and an ax among them. There were no other vehicles, and he briefly wondered if anyone was home, but then he saw the front door was open a crack, and a short woman with mousy brown-blonde hair was peering out at him through the opening.

She came out onto the small porch as Wesson approached the house. There was an almost defiant look in her eyes, and something else he could not quite identify. She left the door open, but whether it was to allow him entrance or to allow herself to flee back inside, Wesson was not sure. She wore a blouse and long-sleeved sweater and a long skirt that ended midcalf. She carried an infant in her right arm, and she half turned away from the approaching policeman as if to shield the child from view. "What do you want?" she said in a breathless but surprisingly strong voice.

Wesson stopped at the foot of the steps. "Mrs. Thompson?"

"My husband is not here."

"Why would you think I came to talk to your husband?"

"Because . . ." Heather Thompson's eyes widened. "Because Gary handles the important . . . uh . . . business . . . things . . ."

"Mrs. Thompson, I am Sergeant Wesson." He did not bother to explain that he was with the RCMP. That much was obvious from his uniform and patrol car. "I'd just like to ask you a couple of questions."

Heather Thompson nodded slightly, but she remained facing him on the porch and did not invite him into the house. Behind her, Wesson could see a perfectly clean and neat living room and a slightly older child peering around a doorway from an equally neat kitchen. "What . . . what about?" she asked.

"Mrs. Thompson, do you know the chain-up area just down the road?"

"Yes."

"In the past couple of days, we found two bodies there, down in the bush. We think they had been there for some time, probably at least a few weeks." Wesson paused, but the woman, who had seemed generally frightened, showed no additional response to this grisly information. "I realize that you can't see the chain-up area from here, but I was wondering if you had seen or heard anything unusual in the last few weeks or months?"

"No," the woman said slowly.

"Did you, for instance, hear a chainsaw?"

"Chainsaw? This is the woods. I can often hear a chainsaw. Gary says it's Hawk . . . a man who does wood carvings. And Gary has a chainsaw to cut wood for the stove."

"Yes, but did you ever hear the sound of a chainsaw coming from the direction of the chain-up area?"

"No, I don't think so."

"Have you ever seen a blonde woman or a man in the area?"

"We don't see many people out here." Wesson paused to see if she would say more. "I see trucks and cars go by, and once in a while there's someone on a bicycle, but they don't stop. I've never talked to any of them."

Cyclists were another possibility, Wesson thought, but they hadn't found any bicycles in the bush. "Where is your husband?" he asked.

The fear was back in the woman's eyes. "He drove into Prince Rupert to do the shopping. He won't be back for about an hour."

"What does he do for a living?"

"He drives a logging truck." The woman nodded in the direction of the driveway.

"Mrs. Thompson, may I ask why you live way out here?"

"It was cheaper, and Gary likes . . . we like the solitude. People don't bother us here."

Wesson started up the step, and the woman jerked and stepped backward. He pulled a card from his pocket. "Mrs. Thompson, if you think of anything that might relate to the two bodies we found, if you remember seeing anybody or hearing anything, or if you ever need anything, please give me a call."

Heather Thompson hesitated, then accepted the card gingerly with two fingers.

"I may come back later when your husband is home. You said an hour or so?"

Heather's hand went to her mouth. "Sergeant," she said in a strange high voice as he turned to go, "could you . . . if you come back . . . don't tell Gary you were here before . . . please?"

Wesson studied the woman's face for a moment, then nodded. "All right."

Mary Pendragon's place, like Gerard Hawkins's, was set far back from the road, reached by a gravel track that wound under the shadows of trees. There was only a very small cleared space around the house, but a big, black old Buick sat at the end of the track. The house was a fair-sized one-story place, with siding that had either been painted black or had turned black with age and mold under the trees.

Getting out of the car, Wesson approached the house slowly. His knock seemed to echo unnaturally through the trees. A moment later, the door slid open silently. Wesson's first impression was that it had opened on its own, but as his eyes adjusted to the murk within, he recognized the outline of a shadowy figure retreating noiselessly down the hall. Entering and shutting the door behind him, he followed the figure a few steps down the hall to a room that was dimly lit by three or four candles. The flickering light revealed only some over-stuffed chairs and a couple of cluttered bookcases. If there were windows, they must have been covered by the heavy, dark tapestries hanging along the back wall.

She was sitting in a dark brown chair facing him, dressed in a long, black layered skirt or dress covered with a black shawl. One chunky bare foot was visible below the hemline, and long, unnaturally black hair hung down over her shoulders. The white of her face contrasted sharply with the clothes, her black lipstick, and her thick black eyebrows. Wesson could also discern large hoop earrings hidden among the hair. If he had had to guess an age, he would have suggested forties or fifties perhaps, middle-aged at least. He sat in another dark brown chair facing her.

"You have come about the bodies." Her thin, husky voice carried clearly in the still air.

"What bodies?"

"The dismembered bodies you found down the road." She raised her hand to her lips and pulled slowly on a long, thin cigar. Smoke floated up in front of her black eyes, which remained fixed on Wesson.

"What do you know about those bodies? Do you know how they got there?"

"They were murdered and cut up and dumped there."

"How do you know?"

"I just know such things."

"Do you know who the bodies are? Do you know who murdered them?"

She pulled again on the cigar, and smoke floated upward, obscuring her eyes. "No."

"Do you know anything about how the bodies got there? Did you see anything going on down at the chain-up area?"

A pause. "No."

"Have you ever seen a blonde woman or a man in this immediate area?"

Another pause. "No."

"You are Mary Pendragon?"

"Yes."

"Is that your real name?"

"What is real?"

"Is it your legal name?"

"What is legal? What do I have to do with law?"

"Have you lived here long?"

"Yes, a long time."

"Do you live alone?"

A dark light came into her eyes, and when she smiled, it only made her seem more eerie. He thought she was not going to answer, but finally she did. "There is no other mortal here to whom you can address your questions."

Again Wesson produced a card and handed it to Mary Pendragon. She took it without glancing at it. "If you think of anything else relating to the murders, please let me know."

She smiled, but it was a smile that radiated cold rather than warmth.

Rising, he turned to the dark hall and stumbled toward the door. She did not follow him. After some fumbling, he found the door handle. As the door swung open, he noticed a small alcove or closet and a faint gleam of polished metal. In the corner of the alcove leaned a black-handled chainsaw and an ax.

Back in the car, Wesson had to maneuver back and forth a few times in order to turn around in the tiny cleared space. Turning back onto the highway, he shivered involuntarily.

Wesson was halfway back to Prince Rupert before he remembered he had intended to go back to see Gary Thompson. Needing a place to turn around, he decided to kill two birds with one stone. *Poor choice of metaphors,* he thought as he pulled into another long driveway leading into the bush.

This driveway led downhill, not up, and opened into a meadow next to a swampy pond. There was a ramshackle three-story house, a number of outbuildings, and a peace sign outlined in rocks, half hidden among the weeds. A man in blue jeans, a faded shirt, and hiking boots was sitting on the porch steps. His unkempt hair and beard were a rusty black. Beside him sat a woman with long, gray-blonde hair wearing a peasant dress.

Wesson stopped the car and got out. "Good morning, Ray, Sun," he said. It didn't seem right to call them Mr. and Mrs. Light. It had never seemed right in any of his conversations with them over the years. They were probably not even married, at least in the legal sense, and certainly not under those names.

The Lights remained seated on the porch. They did not stand, either to welcome or discourage Wesson's presence. They maintained an air of aloofness, as if spiritually they were somewhere else, on a higher plane than Wesson.

"How are you doing?" Wesson asked.

The couple was silent. Wesson was beginning to wonder

if the Lights were out, absent from their bodies. Finally, Ray said in a low, powerful voice that rumbled like thunder in the far distance, "We live in the bosom of nature, and she is a bounteous, nurturing mother."

"We are trying to trace a couple of people," Wesson said. "Can you tell me who is living here with you right now?"

Again there was a long pause. Just when Wesson thought he was going to get no answer, Sun spoke. The conversation was like listening to one of those reporters on a long-distance satellite feed, with long transmission gaps between question and answer. Sun said, "There are no other earthbound children here now." She paused again and added, "But, of course, we are never alone. There are spirits all around us."

Now, where have I heard something like that before? Wesson asked himself silently. He continued out loud, "I am particularly wondering about a man and a blonde woman. Have you seen anyone like that passing through here in the last few months?"

The Lights appeared to be in thought, and the conversation gap was even longer. Ray spoke this time: "Many pass through here. We live on a highway. Many women are blonde. Who can say if they have passed by here? Perhaps the spirits know, but they have not told us."

"We found this man and this woman dead about twenty kilometers east of here. They had been dead quite a long time. Do you know anything about that? Have you seen or heard anything suspicious?"

This time the Lights did not answer, just sat there shaking their heads slightly in unison, like inexpressive puppets.

"There was a woman named Gracie Levasseur living here last fall?" Wesson continued.

"Gracie Levasseur?" It was Sun's turn.

"I believe you called her Shine."

"Ah, Shine," Ray said. "A troubled young woman, she was seeking the light, and it was available to her, as it is to all of us, but in the end she chose not to see it and went down into darkness."

"What do you mean, 'went down into darkness'? Is she dead? Did you kill her?"

In spite of the sudden sharpness of Wesson's question, Ray again paused before answering in the same monotonous rumble. "I did not kill her. She merely returned to the darkness of the outside world. Your world."

"*You* did not kill her? Did Sun?"

Again a pause before Ray spoke. "Sun is full of light. She could not perform a deed of darkness."

"When did Shine leave here?"

Ray continued to speak. He spread his hands. "What is time? It was many moons ago, about the time the snow came."

"How did she leave? Did she say where she was going?"

"She just got up and left one morning very early, while the world was sleeping, without saying a word." It was Sun this time. "That is how we know she went out into darkness."

"How do you know she left if it was still dark?"

"I saw her go," Sun said.

"How, if it was dark?"

"Those who live in the light can see in the darkness," Ray answered. Wesson wondered how Sun knew that it was Ray who would answer this question. There were no visible signs of communication between them, but they always seemed to know whose turn it was. Perhaps they were communing privately in the pauses.

"Which direction did she go when she left?"

"Up the long lane," Sun answered. Wesson thought she was going to leave him with this unhelpful answer, but then she added, "And she turned toward the east."

45

"Was she alone? Did anyone go with her?"

"There was no visible presence with her; no earthbound creature went with her. What spirits accompanied her—who can say?"

Who indeed? thought Wesson. "Could she have met someone? Was there someone waiting for her? Up at the highway, perhaps?"

"I saw no one else."

"There was a young man living here at the time, and also a young woman. I believe you called them Moon and Lucid."

"Yes, they left also."

"When?"

Again Ray spread out his hands.

"Did they leave when Shine left?"

"No. It was later, a moon or two, in midwinter."

"Did they leave together?"

"Yes."

"That left the two of you living here alone?"

"Yes. No one else has lived here since."

Wesson wasn't sure he believed that. He wasn't sure the Lights would know or remember if anyone else had been living there. In any case, the conversation was going nowhere. Wesson said, "If you do think of anything else, if you discover anything else, you will let me know?" He did not bother handing them a card. He was certain they would never be able to find it if they needed it.

The Lights did remain silent this time, sitting on the porch, heads stretched forward, like two sphinxes. He got into his car and drove back out the lane. As he was about to turn back onto the highway going east, he paused and looked back at the house. He could not see it through the trees. He had not seen an ax or a chainsaw at this place, but that meant nothing. Every house in the area had them, just as surely as

46

they had roofs and doors and stoves. He thought again of the Lights and pondered how light could seem so dark.

Going east again, Wesson headed back to Gary Thompson's place. This time, a dirty green pickup truck sat in the driveway. Wesson saw a shadow at a window, and then a blond, muscular man of medium height came out the door. He met Wesson halfway between the house and the car, held out his hand, and smiled broadly. "Good afternoon, Officer. Can I help you?"

"Mr. Thompson?" Wesson asked as they shook hands.

"Yes, Gary Thompson."

"I am Sergeant Wesson with the Prince Rupert RCMP. I was wondering if you had seen any unusual activity down by the chain-up area near here in the past few months."

"No, can't say that I have."

"Have you heard anything unusual—shouting, screams, a chainsaw?"

"No, I don't remember anything. Well, chainsaws, but that's not unusual around here—our neighbor uses them in his wood carving. Why do you ask?"

"The bodies of two people were discovered in the bush below the chain-up area. The bodies had probably been there for some time, possibly a few weeks or more."

"Bodies? Is there a serial killer out here somewhere? Are my wife and kids safe? They're often here alone when I'm away working."

"At this point, we have no reason to believe there is a serial killer or that your family is in any danger. We don't know a great deal at this point, to be honest. But, if you are worried, why do you live way out here?"

"It is cheaper and closer to where I work—I drive a logging truck. And my wife prefers the solitude, where people are not bothering her all the time."

"The bodies we found—one was a man and the other a blonde woman. Have you seen anyone like that?"

"No, not really."

Wesson handed over two of his business cards. "If you or your wife think of anything else, or if you have any concerns, will you get in touch with me?"

"I will do that." Gary smiled again. "Thanks for coming and warning us about this."

Wesson silently handed out packets of pages to his task force, which had assembled in one of the station's two small conference rooms. "These are copies of the autopsy reports and some preliminary forensics," he said. It was eight o'clock on Saturday night, and he had spent the last couple of hours reading them.

"What's in them?" Leblanc wanted to know.

"I expect you to read them all," Wesson said, then relented. "The bottom line is that there are two victims—"

"You're sure this time?" It was Trent Simmons, making the kind of ill-advised comment that could get him sent back to traffic patrol and kept there for a long time.

"Yes," Wesson said evenly, "we're sure." Picking up the report, he read the summary that was couched in a style of public pronouncements familiar to Canadians ever since the switch to the metric system. Measurements were given in pounds, feet, and inches for older members of the public and in kilograms and meters for younger people. "The first victim is a woman in her twenties, one-point-seven meters tall—that's five foot seven—shoulder-length blonde hair, about sixty-three kilograms or one hundred forty pounds, not a virgin. The other is a male, dark hair, probably in his thirties, one-point-seven-five meters or five-nine, seventy-five kilograms or one hundred sixty-five pounds. Death occurred probably several months ago. Cause of death probably due to a blow to the head by a sharp object, perhaps something like an ice pick, but the bodies have deteriorated to the point that the shape of the wound is no longer clearly discernible. The bodies were cut up by a high-speed saw and the body parts frozen immediately afterward, remaining frozen for some time, probably until about two weeks ago."

"That would be about the time the snow melted up there among the trees?" Lynn Johnson asked.

Wesson shrugged. "I guess so. Evidently bodies that have been frozen deteriorate much more quickly once they thaw out."

There was a long silence as the enormity of the crimes sank in. Even for officers who had seen previous murder victims and grisly carnage in automobile accidents, the deliberation and cold-blooded cruelty of these deaths was chilling. At last, Archbold shook himself and observed, "Cut up with a high-speed saw and frozen right afterward—that doesn't narrow it down much. Bodies dumped up there in winter would freeze immediately, and just about everybody up here has a chainsaw."

"Precisely," said Wesson.

"The murder weapon might be more unique."

"Maybe, but forensics couldn't be precise about it. Could be an ice pick or a knife or a chisel or just about anything of that type. Good thing the bodies were frozen for a few months, or they wouldn't even reveal that much."

"Any trace fibers?" Lynn Johnson asked.

"Very little. Some found in the area, might or might not be from the bodies. We have DNA evidence and dental impressions, of course, but we would need something to compare them to. No fingerprints, as all the fingers were mangled."

"A professional hit?" asked Archbold.

"Maybe, but a man and a woman? Not usual. And the mafia isn't a big presence in the Prince Rupert area. Any other ideas?"

"A serial killer?" Lynn Johnson spoke the words the others had been avoiding. "Were they killed at the same time or separately?"

"About the same time. It's not conclusive."

"Two bodies, several months ago—that's when the two hunters disappeared," Archbold suggested.

"But not even several years in the open could turn two men in their late fifties into a blonde woman in her twenties and a man in his thirties."

"I checked, and the two hunters are still missing, by the way," Leblanc put in.

"What about Gracie Levasseur?" Johnson asked. "The age, hair, and height are right."

"I checked on her too," Leblanc said. "She is still missing."

"See if they can track down a DNA sample or dental records."

"I'll work on it."

"Who would the other one be then?" Johnson asked. "What was the name of that other man at Ray and Sun's place?"

"Luther Malone, a.k.a. Moon," Leblanc said.

"Could he be the other body?"

"Maybe. He was about the right age—thirty-one, I think."

Wesson stated, "I was out there this afternoon. Ray and Sun told me that Luther Malone and Amber Long left together about two months after the woman we think may have been Gracie Levasseur. Of course, given Ray's and Sun's grasp of details, it might have been two weeks."

"We know there was at least some time between," Archbold said, "because when we went looking for Gracie a couple of weeks later, Malone and Long were still there and Gracie was not."

"Is it possible," Johnson asked, "that the two of them might have met up with Gracie after she left?"

"How?" Archbold asked. "Remember, it was winter. Where was Gracie in the meantime?"

"Who knows?" Johnson said. "Maybe she went away and came back."

"So our bodies would be Gracie Levasseur and Luther Malone?" Wesson suggested.

"Makes sense," Johnson said.

"Then who killed them?"

Johnson pondered a moment. "I guess that leaves Amber Long."

"Why would she do it?"

"Jealousy?"

"A love triangle? That's possible," Wesson said. "I'm still uncomfortable with the two-month gap. Of course, Ray and Sun might have lied about Gracie leaving first."

"Maybe Gracie was killed first and Malone a month or two later," Johnson said. "Gracie might even have been killed while all three were still together at Ray and Sun's place. Even if they were dumped in the same place two months apart, the bodies would still start to decompose at the same time when they thawed out in the spring."

"Ray and Sun might have done it," Archbold suggested. "Maybe they killed all three and we haven't found Amber Long's body yet."

"You want me to check on all three of them, right?" Leblanc asked Wesson.

"Yes."

There was a silence. Wesson went on. "Forensics is working on reconstructions of the faces and will send us sketches hopefully by late tomorrow. Then I'll call a news conference so we can get the photos spread across Canada and the U.S. Maybe somebody will recognize them."

"A bit late for the news conference, I think," said Simmons.

"What do you mean?" Wesson asked.

"Haven't you seen today's Vancouver paper?"

"No," Wesson said. "I've been working."

Simmons jumped to his feet, went out into the outer office, and came back with a newspaper, which he folded open and dropped onto the desk. The headline glared up at Wesson: "B.C. chainsaw killer? Police find dismembered bodies near Prince Rupert."

"Wow. That's restrained," Leblanc said. "Ought to help prevent panic in the community."

"How did they know about the chainsaw?" Wesson asked.

"A leak from the lab in Vancouver?" suggested Johnson.

"Come on," Archbold insisted. "They're guessing. They saw the forensics teams bring the second body up in pieces from the chain-up area. The headline's obviously referring to the movie."

"What movie?" Wesson asked.

The Texas Chainsaw Massacre," Leblanc said. "It's a classic. Haven't you seen it?"

Wesson shook his head. "I don't see many movies."

"Maybe somebody else up here has," Archbold suggested.

"A copycat?"

"This isn't a movie," Johnson said softly.

Chapter 5

SUNDAY, MAY 23

"You getting up?"

Wesson rolled over and groaned. "No," he moaned. "I'm tired."

"But you promised this week you'd go—"

"That was before two people got themselves murdered."

"All the more reason to go to church, get perspective . . ."

"And I had to work three twelve-hour days in a row."

Wesson's wife, Sandy, turned and walked out of the bedroom.

Wesson closed his eyes again and burrowed deeper under the covers. A few months ago, Sandy had suddenly begun attending a small church, and ever since then she had been nagging him to come too. He didn't know what had gotten into her, but so far he had resisted, and he hoped she would soon forget about the whole thing. He wasn't exactly a churchgoing man in the first place, and his weariness was real. It wasn't just the long hours he had been working. The truth was he hadn't slept well the last few nights. Several times visions of human bodies being torn apart by whirling chainsaws had jerked him back into sweat-soaked consciousness. At a time like this, real-life matters like public safety seemed more important than church.

At three, Wesson's quiet Sunday at home was shattered by the ringing of the telephone.

"Wesson," he said into the receiver.

"Sergeant, this is Simmons at the station. I'm sorry to bother you on your day off, but the facial-reconstruction drawings for the two bodies just arrived from Vancouver. I thought you'd like to know."

"Thanks. I'll be in soon. Call a news conference for six."

"What?" Calling news conferences was something beyond Simmons's experience. There was only one main newspaper in town, and when Marge Oldham wanted to know something, she usually just called the station.

"Call Marge at home and tell her to come to the station at six o'clock this evening. Tell her I'll give her an update on the two bodies that were found. I think the stringer and the Vancouver television reporter are still in town, probably staying at the Maple Leaves Motel. They gave me their business cards yesterday, and I tacked them up on the bulletin board in my office. Phone them and tell them the same thing you told Marge. Then make some copies of the drawings—"

"But how . . . ? I mean, Laura downloaded the e-mail but then went home sick, and I'm handling reception at the moment, and I don't—"

"Phone Mildred at home. Ask her to come in and make a couple of dozen prints and a half-dozen CD copies of the drawings so we can give them out to the press."

"Oh."

When Wesson pushed the door open, it stuck halfway. Squeezing around the half-open door, he realized the problem. The tiny station was filled with bodies. At least these were *live* bodies. Pushing his way through to the doorway of the private office, he turned and surveyed those who were there. Marge Oldham with her tight gray hair and square jaw was a far more formidable reporter than the twenty-two-year-old Skip Jackson. Wesson recognized Jason Thuringer, the Vancouver newspaper stringer, and Melanie Grayson, the Vancouver TV reporter. There was also a new reporter—a short Asian man in his thirties—and two men in blue jeans holding portable TV cameras on their shoulders. Wesson stared at the Asian man.

"Jordan Leung, Canadian Broadcasting Corporation," Mildred murmured, coming up beside him. "They've all been here since five thirty."

Wesson nodded, gestured with his head, and then retreated into the private office. Mildred followed, shut the door, and spread a file folder on the desk in front of him. Two drawings stared up at him. One was the round face of a man in his thirties, clean shaven, with dark hair. The other, the woman, had a sharp nose, full lips, large eyes, and shoulder-length blonde hair. Wesson didn't recognize either one of them, but he was never impressed by these computerized drawings anyway. They looked somewhat inhuman, like nobody, but also in a sense like just about anybody—too generic or lifeless to really remind you of the person they were supposed to represent.

"Do you have the hard copies and the CDs for the press?"

"Of course," Mildred replied.

"I wasn't sure Simmons would get the message right. Did any new information come in with these?"

"No."

"These things came through pretty quick."

"Using the computers apparently speeds up the process quite a bit."

"Did Vancouver say if they had tried to match these reconstructions with any photos of missing people?"

"They didn't say, but if they had any hot leads, I'm sure they would have told us."

"Yeah, I'm sure." Wesson was sarcastic. Communications in the RCMP weren't always what they could be.

He nodded to Mildred and then put in a call to Inspector Travis. Travis was out, of course, it being Sunday, but he got Sergeant Trahota, a supercilious RCMP bureaucrat based at the regional headquarters in Vancouver.

"This is Sergeant Wesson in Prince Rupert. I just got the computer drawings from Vancouver. I was wondering if you guys had matched them to any missing persons?"

"We're checking, but nothing obvious so far. Why would you expect us to do this anyway? Travis says you want to handle the investigation."

"Yeah, but the missing-persons check is headquarters routine."

"Well, we haven't found anything. How about you?"

"We're still checking and interviewing. I'll go out again tomorrow with the drawings, but so far nothing that looks promising. Do you think Travis would object if I gave the drawings out to the press, held a press conference?" Wesson realized too late that he should have asked headquarters about this first. Normally headquarters didn't care what information he gave to Marge Oldham, but this was a case that was likely to generate national attention.

"Thanks for asking." Trahota was far better at sarcasm than Wesson. "Travis says that's obviously something you've decided to handle as well. Says you looked real cool on TV."

"I was on TV?"

"Don't you have television up there? It was on the Vancouver news. I thought you looked like a fumbling idiot, but Travis wants to let you mess things up on your own."

Wesson thought back to the rather confused impromptu news conference he had given at the chain-up area. It probably wasn't his finest hour. As a headquarters staff officer, Trahota had been interviewed on television dozens of times.

"Thanks," Wesson said and hung up.

He went to the door and called Mildred in again. Holding the door closed for a second, he said, "Mildred, I want you to give a hard copy and a CD to each of the reporters. Later, you're going to have to make more hard copies. I want each of our officers to have a copy, and the task force will need more. You'll also need some to send out to any other media who ask." He started to open the door, and she turned to go. "And, Mildred, thanks for coming in on a Sunday."

Mildred shrugged, obviously thinking, *Better late than never*. She often claimed her skills were taken for granted, but Wesson knew she was a remarkable woman. On her own initiative, she had gone to Prince George and earned a two-year certificate in office procedures and computer skills as well as a prelaw B.A. from the University of Northern British Columbia —the first Native woman to graduate from that program. She went to her desk and began handing around the drawings.

"Mildred is—" Wesson blinked as the camera lights flashed on. "These are reconstructions of the faces of the two bodies we found last week at the chain-up area out on the highway. They are computer-assisted reproductions of the faces. We have not yet identified either of the victims, so any help you or your readers—or listeners—can give us would be appreciated. Anyone who may recognize one of the victims should contact the Prince Rupert RCMP. The one is a male, midthirties, dark hair, brown eyes, approximately one-point-seven-five meters, five foot nine, seventy-five kilograms, one hundred sixty-five pounds. The other is a woman in her twenties, shoulder-length blonde hair, eyes indeterminate but probably blue, one-point-seven meters, five foot seven, about sixty-three kilograms, one hundred forty pounds. We think the bodies were out there several months."

"Why didn't you give us actual photos?" Melanie Grayson asked.

"The bodies were somewhat decomposed, and photos wouldn't have shown as much as the reproductions."

"Were the bodies mutilated, cut up?" she shot back.

"The bodies were dismembered to some extent, but—"

"Are we dealing with a chainsaw murderer here?" Jordan Leung inserted, obviously concerned that his voice be on the tape.

"It's too early to say that. We do suspect foul play, but we don't know exactly how these people died."

"Don't you know cause of death?"

"We have probable cause of death, but we are not releasing that information—"

"Is there someone wandering around in the woods cutting innocent people to pieces with a chainsaw?" Melanie Grayson this time. "Are other people at risk?"

"We have no indication there is a chainsaw murderer out there." Wesson was trying unsuccessfully to put sarcasm into his voice. "We have no reason to think anyone else is in danger."

"But do you know?"

"Well, no, but these have been there several months, and we haven't found any more bodies."

"Did you look?"

"We searched the area very thoroughly."

"What about other areas? Did you search the entire woods?"

"The entire woods? We're talking thousands of hectares of rainforest out there—"

"How did you find the first bodies?"

"First bodies? We don't know that there are any—"

"That wasn't the question. How did you find the first bodies?"

"The bodies were first discovered by a motorist who stopped at the chain-up area."

"Who is the motorist? What's his name?"

"We're not releasing that information."

"Is he a suspect?"

"No."

A couple of other questions were shouted out, but Wesson held up his hand. "That's all the information we have at this time. I will let you know if we have any other information to release."

There would have been more questions, but Wesson ducked back into the private office and shut the door. A few seconds later, he opened it again. "And don't ask our dispatcher any questions, or I'll arrest you for obstructing a police investigation."

The assembled reporters dispersed with considerable reluctance and grumbling. Marge, the last one out, paused in the doorway and looked back at Wesson.

"No, Marge, not even for you. We just don't know any more."

The rain had cleared, and John Smyth had a good view of the city as the plane circled and descended toward the runway on the western edge of Winnipeg. He sighed. It had been another tiring convention, and, after two days in Calgary, he was glad to be coming home—glad also that everything he saw from the window was peaceful and normal. The bank towers still dominated the center of the city, and off to one side loomed the stone towers of Winnipeg Cold Storage. The latter looked as they had looked for as long as Smyth could remember—except for the flame of a bright orange logo proclaiming "Winnipack." That had only been there the past five years. Smyth knew—in fact, all Winnipeg was talking about—the story behind that logo.

Businessman Grant Parkinson had arrived from the U.S., taken over a bankrupt meatpacking plant as well as the adjacent cold storage towers, and performed what many termed a modern miracle—although John Smyth preferred to reserve the term *miracle* for more directly discernible acts of the Almighty. Within a year, Winnipack was making a profit. Within two years, the company was selling its frozen specialty meat products in overseas markets. When Canadian railroads had been unable to guarantee prompt delivery, Parkinson had acquired a fleet of refrigerator trucks and established his own delivery system. When shipping charges at Canada's main West Coast port, Vancouver, had become too high, he had begun shipping his products out through the smaller northern port of Prince Rupert.

Parkinson's drive and vision had made Winnipack what it was. What Grant Parkinson envisioned, Grant Parkinson achieved. Using upgraded machinery, carefully designed employee incentives, rigid quality controls, slick and intensive advertising, and that contemporary orange logo, Winnipack had almost overnight built a reputation for remarkably high quality at a remarkably reasonable price. His success story had gained much attention, perhaps because such unqualified success was a rarity in a city that was sometimes described as "gently declining."

And all of it had been achieved by Grant Parkinson's remarkable dedication to his business. He had taken an interest in every aspect of the company. It was said that he sometimes worked in the meatpacking plant itself to get orders out on time during busy seasons, ensure quality control, and keep an eye on the business from the bottom up. Perhaps Parkinson was too dedicated to his work, Smyth reflected. As an evangelical Christian, Smyth valued marriage very highly—and rumor had it that two months ago, in the middle of all that success, Parkinson's wife had left him and moved back to the States.

Smyth understood hard work. As an editor, he had a busy schedule with constant deadlines, but he always made time for Ruby and his children. Parkinson evidently had no children, and Smyth had four of them. The more he thought about it, Smyth reflected, he was a far richer man than Grant Parkinson.

The taxi bounced once more over the potholes of inner-city Winnipeg and deposited John Smyth in front of a gray stucco story-and-a-half house fronted by a white picket fence. As he pulled his suitcase out of the taxi's trunk, Smyth glanced at the living room picture window. Ruby was not there watching for him. He walked up the sidewalk, climbed the steps, pushed open the front door, and set his bags down in the hall. He was immediately surrounded by four children who appeared as if by magic from the four corners of the house. This was more like it. Then Ruby appeared in the living room doorway, the sun from the picture window causing her red hair to shine like a flame. Smiling, she pushed through the children and gave her husband a big hug and kiss.

Behind her, through the haze of her red hair, Smyth caught sight of another woman sitting primly on the living room sofa, her bright white hair contrasting sharply with her tasteful dark-blue dress. Company. Smyth's heart groaned, even as his mouth smiled. The last thing he wanted after a weekend convention was having to sit and make polite conversation with a visitor.

The woman rose and advanced toward the huddle of the Smyths. "Hello, John," she said. "Welcome back." The white hair framed a square, pale face with dark brown eyes and a jutting chin.

"I invited Elvira over after the potluck lunch at church," Ruby said. "She's staying for supper."

"Oh, good," John Smyth said brightly.

Elvira had stayed until about eight thirty and then driven herself home. The conversation had been polite but mundane. John had the feeling that the real conversation may have taken place before he arrived and that Elvira was staying on out of politeness or some other unfathomable reason.

"I'm sorry, John," Ruby said when she had gone. "Elvira's having a hard time right now, and I thought she just needed to be with someone."

Elvira was part of a home Bible study or "care group" led by the Smyths. This was a group of about a dozen people from their church who met once a week in each other's homes. The purpose, the people at the church said, was "fellowship" or, if they were feeling particularly theological, *koinonia,* but most other people would call it "friendship." The group members prayed together and studied the Bible, but they also just talked to each other ("shared" was what they called it) and tried to support each other with whatever problems they were facing.

"Jake hasn't turned up yet, then?"

"No," Ruby answered. "Two months ago was the last time she saw him."

"She's heard nothing?"

"Nothing. And the police don't have any new leads."

"Did she talk about why he took off like that or where he might be now?"

"John, she didn't talk about that. She doesn't. She's a very private woman, and I don't think she shares her feelings easily. Plus she seems to be—well, in denial or something. Today she mostly just talked about the good times—her daily life with John, how he would take her out to lunch on Sunday and open the car door for her, raising their kids. She was three or four years older than Jake. Did you know that? She said he always treated her with respect and then joked with her about it, saying he treated her that way because she was an 'older woman.' It must be awful, after thirty-seven years of marriage, for him to just up and leave . . ."

There was a pause. "John," she said, "you won't ever do that, will you?"

"No," John promised and put his arms around her. "I don't have as much money as Jake Rempel. I couldn't afford it."

Chapter 6

MONDAY, MAY 24

Monday morning began with another meeting of the Prince Rupert RCMP task force. Wesson handed out copies of the facial reconstructions. The officers looked silently at the faces of two people who had been brutally murdered.

"Pierre," Wesson said, turning to Leblanc, "you keep working the missing-persons angle. I am going to go back and see the people who live near the chain-up area and drop in to see Bear Miniwac—"

"That ought to be fun," Leblanc mumbled.

Wesson ignored the interruption. "Archie, when you come on shift this evening, I want you to begin house-to-house inquiries of every place between Prince Rupert and Terrace."

Archbold nodded and stretched his long, thin legs. "Sure," he said. "That's only about a hundred fifty kilometers of highway."

"Lynn," Wesson continued, "you and the others can begin house-to-house inquiries in Prince Rupert. If Pierre or Archie need any help, they can pull you in as needed. Okay?"

A half hour later, Wesson turned into the driveway that led down to Ray and Sun Light's ramshackle three-story house. No one seemed to be around. Wesson got out of the car, mounted the steps to the porch, and knocked on the door. A few moments later, he heard shuffling feet inside. A few moments later still, the door opened. Sun Light wore the same peasant dress from two days before, but with a long apron over it. She pushed a strand of stringy gray-blonde hair out of her eyes.

"Good morning, Sun," Wesson said.

"Good morning." Sun Light seemed hesitant, faded somehow, as if she were only half there without Ray present.

"Sun, I would like you to look at these two pictures. These are computer reconstructions of the faces of the two bodies we found at the chain-up area. Do they look at all familiar to you?"

Sun took the two pictures and looked them over slowly. Finally, she said, "No, I don't think I've ever seen them before."

"This one couldn't be Gracie Levasseur, for instance?"

"Gracie? Gracie who?"

"Is it Shine, then?"

Sun was silent for a moment, then said, "No, it's not Shine."

"Are you sure?"

"Yes."

"How about the other photo? Could that be Luther Malone—Moon?"

"No," she said without looking at the photo.

"Is Ray around?"

"Ray? No, he's . . . out for a walk in the woods."

Wesson didn't believe that. Ray was more likely out tending his marijuana patch. But it was no use pushing the point. "Thanks, Sun. Have a good day."

Sun brightened. "Oh, I always have a good day."

It was an impressive log structure about one hundred twenty-five feet long, designed by a company near Vancouver, shipped to Prince Rupert, and assembled there—all at government expense—after a bidding process in which several large companies approved by the government had participated. Standing on the porch of this "authentic" band office was a barrel-chested, middle-aged Native man, his dark face set in a scowl. Wesson pulled the patrol car to a stop in front of the building and got out.

"Good morning, Bear," he said.

The other man nodded almost imperceptibly but did not speak.

Wesson walked up to him and held out the two drawings. "Last week, we found two bodies by the chain-up area on the highway about fifteen kilometers east of here. They had been there for several months. These are computer reconstructions of their faces. I was wondering if you or any of your people might have seen them."

Bear remained standing silently for a long time. Finally, he spoke. "Whenever there is trouble in white society, you come and blame it on us."

"That's not true, Bear. We're not blaming your people. We just know they are often in the woods and along the highway, and we just wondered if they might have seen something. We're asking everyone in town and along the highway. We're doing a thorough investigation."

"A thorough investigation? And when I reported my daughter missing, did you do a thorough investigation?"

Wesson sighed. "We had no starting point. She went missing somewhere between here and Vancouver. We put a lot of hours into looking for her."

"As many hours as if she had been a blonde white woman?"

"Yes," Wesson insisted. "In fact, that's one of the other reasons I came out here. I wanted to follow up with you, to see if your daughter has shown up. Have you heard anything more from her or about her?"

"No," Bear said abruptly. He grabbed the drawings.

At that moment, laughter erupted around the side of the building, and both men stood listening. A few moments later, a half-dozen black-haired teenaged boys shuffled around the side of the building, laughing and giggling. Several of them carried plastic bags with a reddish liquid in them. Two of them carried rifles, and most of them had knives. Seeing the Mountie, they stopped.

The leader, a younger, thinner Bear, swaggered forward. "Look, it's a policeman!" he called. The boys behind him sniggered. "What ya doin' here, Mr. White Policeman? This is our land. We're going hunting. We got rights to hunt anything we like anytime we like." He waved the rifle vaguely in Wesson's direction. The boys sniggered again. The two men glowered at him. "What we gonna hunt? Maybe we hunt some white rabbits." The boys giggled.

"Come here, Daniel," Wesson said.

The boy hesitated, glanced at his father, and came slowly forward. Wesson reached into the car and pulled out two more drawings. He handed the drawings to Daniel. "Do you remember seeing either of these two people in the area maybe several months ago?"

68

Daniel looked at the drawings and shrugged. "No. White people all look alike to me."

"How about your friends?"

Daniel passed the drawings back to the other boys, who gathered in a circle, looking at the pictures and shaking their heads. Wesson glanced at Daniel and back at the other boys. Somewhere in the circle, the drawings had disappeared. The boys stood in an irregular semicircle, smirking at Wesson.

"How about last year when you stole that truck out on the highway?"

"I never stole a truck," Daniel said petulantly.

"He did not steal a truck," Bear said angrily.

Wesson ignored him. "These two people were found dead in the bush near the chain-up area on the highway about fifteen kilometers east of here. They apparently died several months ago. Any of you know anything about that?"

The boys had become quiet and serious. They stood there gently shaking their heads and staring at Wesson.

"If any of you remember anything or hear of anything, let me or Mr. Miniwac know, okay?"

The boys stood silent, staring.

"Bear, do you recognize the faces?"

The Native said nothing but slowly moved his head from side to side.

"Thank you for looking," Wesson said. "I'd appreciate it if you passed the drawings around among your people. Maybe somebody saw or heard something." He stood for a moment, nodded at Bear, and got back into his cruiser.

Bear nodded once more and stood without moving as Wesson started the engine and drove away.

This time, Wesson decided to start with the most distant of the three places and work backward. This time he got through the chain-link gate and into the yard without being noticed from the house. As he knocked on the door, he thought he caught a half-strangled sound, as if someone was crying. It was almost a full minute before Heather Thompson peeked out through the front drapes and a few more moments before she came to the door. She was dressed more or less as before. She did not speak.

Wesson said, "I am sorry to bother you again, Mrs. Thompson. We now have some pictures of the two people whose bodies we found at the chain-up area. I wonder if you would mind looking at them to see if you recognize them."

She nodded. Wesson handed the pictures over and added, "These are computer reconstructions based on the bone structure of the skull. The people might have looked some-what different—different hairstyles, for instance, maybe slightly different features. The woman is about five foot seven and in her twenties, the man about five foot nine and in his thirties. Do either of them look at all familiar to you?"

"No," Heather answered. "I don't think I've seen them." She handed the pictures back.

"Thank you, Mrs. Thompson," said Wesson. "If you do re-member anything or think of anything, please let me know. Another officer will come out tonight to talk to Gary."

"Thank you," she said and half smiled.

Wesson turned to go, then turned back. "Mrs. Thompson, do you still have the card I gave you?"

She nodded.

"Mrs. Thompson, if you ever need anything—if you ever get afraid living way out here or you want to get away or you need a place to run to and hide, you can call me anytime."

She looked at him carefully for a while, then said, "Hide from the man who murdered those people at the chain-up area, you mean?"

70

"That . . . and for any other reason."

"Thank you," she said again.

The bear was slowly emerging from the wood—his head first, then his right front paw, raised and about to strike. Gerard Hawkins, busy with the chainsaw, had apparently not heard Wesson drive in. Wesson watched fascinated for a few moments, then walked around into Hawkins's line of vision. Hawkins lowered the chainsaw and let it idle but did not shut it off.

"Good morning, Mr. Hawkins," Wesson said over the burr of the idling saw. "I have some drawings of the faces of the two people we found down by the chain-up area. Would you mind looking at them?"

Hawkins nodded and stepped away from the wood, the saw still idling in his hand. He looked at the two pictures Wesson held out but did not touch them.

"Do you recognize either of these two people?" Wesson began, aware that he was beginning to lapse into singsong repetition. "These are computer reconstructions, so they might have looked somewhat different—different hairstyles, perhaps somewhat different features."

"Nope." Hawkins shook his head. "Never saw either of 'em before." He turned back to the wood sculpture and began refining the detail on the upraised paw.

"Mr. Hawkins," Wesson shouted over the louder whine of the saw, "do you live alone?"

There was no jerk of the hands, but the saw swiftly slid upward and the severed paw arced through the air, landing at Wesson's feet. Both men stood awestruck at the desecration of the magnificent beast. After what seemed an eternity, Hawkins's hand relaxed and the saw subsided to a quiet whirr, then empty silence. Both continued to stare at each other.

"I'm very sorry," Wesson began. "I didn't mean—"

"Yeah," Hawkins said.

"Yeah?"

"Yeah, I live alone. What else did you expect?"

"Have you always lived alone?"

"Here, yeah."

"How long have you lived here?"

"'Bout three years." Hawkins's eyes became distant. "Useless kids."

"What?"

"Huh?" Hawkins seemed confused for a moment, stumbled over his words, and finally got out. "If you're looking for who killed them folks, it was probably a gang of kids."

"Kids?"

"A gang of teenagers, young punks."

"Why do you say that?"

"You ever been down in the Cariboo?" Hawkins asked.

Wesson nodded. He was familiar with the open ranch country a few hundred kilometers to the south.

"Kids are like dogs. One dog on his own can be loyal and affectionate, but put a bunch of 'em together, the pack mentality takes over and they start killin' cattle. Same with kids. On his own, a kid might be awkward and stupid, but he ain't dangerous. Put a bunch of 'em together, though, and they're a gang, howlin' at the moon and pushin' each other into trouble. They start feelin' brave and mean, and first thing you know they've killed somebody or destroyed something or wrecked something else. Most crimes are done by gangs of young punks. Down in the Cariboo, they got a rule. You see one dog runnin' loose, you leave 'im alone. You see two or more dogs together, you shoot 'em on sight. They ought to do the same thing with kids."

There was a long, awkward pause. "Is that what you did?"

Wesson asked softly. "Saw a couple of teenagers and killed them on sight?" He knew he was fishing. The bodies weren't even close to being teenagers. But he thought the accusation might solicit a telling reaction.

Hawkins didn't rise to the bait. "Nope. Didn't see none. Might have done something if I had, but I didn't." Hawkins turned his back on Wesson and began studying the damage to the bear.

Without a word, Wesson got into his car and drove off.

Wesson couldn't have said why he left Mary Pendragon till last. His orderly mind might have argued that he was visiting the people in the order in which they were spread out along the highway. But why not visit her first? The truth was that she made him vaguely uneasy—uneasy in a sense that the more obviously powerful Gerard Hawkins did not.

Black smoke was curling from the chimney of the black house. It was strange how the small shaded space around this house felt colder than anywhere else he had been today. When he knocked on the door, it creaked open as before, and the woman led him once more into the dark recess of the interior. Dim candles cast dark shadows on the walls in a macabre dance.

"You have come on behalf of the dead," she said. "You do not have all of them. The spirits have the rest."

Wesson was not sure how to respond to that. He pulled two pictures out of an envelope, handed them to her, and began his litany once more.

She stared intently at the pictures. Wesson had a fleeting mental image of her eyes burning holes through the faces. "No," she said at length. "These two are unknown to me."

She said nothing else, nor did Wesson. It had been a simple, routine inquiry, like hundreds he had conducted. Yet afterward, he could not remember how long he had sat there, nor could he recall leaving the house and returning to his cruiser. His first clear recollection was of driving swiftly back down the highway toward Prince Rupert.

Mildred was watching expectantly as Wesson came through the door.

"Good news?" he said.

"We have positive identifications from the pictures distributed by the media."

"Really?"

"Yes, seventeen of them."

"What?"

"Seventeen people have called in today saying they know who the victims are."

"Well, who are they?"

"That depends on which caller you ask. We have seventeen different identities."

"Take down all the information they give you. Pass it on to Leblanc and have him check them out. It will probably mean getting DNA samples and sending them to Vancouver to check for matches."

"That's what I thought."

The phone rang again.

"John," Ruby Smyth asked her husband that evening, "did you see the story in the newspaper about them finding two dismembered bodies near Prince Rupert? That's where you're going next weekend, right?"

"Yes, I saw it. Those two faces looked so sad," John Smyth replied.

"But you'll be driving along that highway. Please be careful."

"Ruby, I'm always careful. People get murdered in Winnipeg too, and you don't tell me to be careful every time I go to work in the morning. I'm going there to write about the renewal at the Prince Rupert Grace Church, not to get mixed up in a murder. I promise I'll stay safe."

"You know you can't promise that."

"I know, but God can."

"Sure he can. But has he?"

It was late at night when the phone rang.

"Wesson."

"Boss, it's Archie. You wanted me to check in when I got back."

"Yes, what did you find out?"

"I started at the edge of town and stopped at every place from there to the chain-up area—that's as far as I got. Nobody remembers seeing either of those two or anything suspicious. I'm not too impressed with these computer drawings, though. They all end up looking like Bill Gates."

"It's routine, but it has to be done. Tomorrow evening you can start working east from the chain-up area. Did you see Gary Thompson?"

"Yeah. The last place I stopped."

"How did he strike you?"

"He didn't strike me, but I wouldn't have been surprised if he had. He was friendly enough—didn't recognize either of the two victims, by the way—but there's something not right there."

"Did you see Heather Thompson?"

"No, and I didn't ask about her either."

"Good. Call me again tomorrow."

Chapter 7

TUESDAY, MAY 25

Tuesday was taken up with Archbold, Johnson, and Simmons continuing the door-to-door inquiries and Leblanc and Rumple responding to and checking out the "positive identifications" that were flowing into the station and that, by day's end, had reached thirty-nine. Wesson tried to give some encouragement to both endeavors, field inquiries from the media, and catch up on overdue administrative work.

He didn't get nearly as much accomplished as he had hoped.

Tuesday night was Bible study night for John and Ruby Smyth. The participants took turns hosting the study in their homes, and this Tuesday night was John and Ruby's turn. After some informal conversation over coffee and cake, John Smyth said a brief prayer and then began to read aloud from the Bible: "Now listen, you who say, 'Today or tomorrow we will go to this or that city, spend a year there, carry on business and make money.' Why, you do not even know what will happen tomorrow. What is your life? You are a mist that appears for a little while and then vanishes. Instead, you ought to say, 'If it is the Lord's will, we will live and do—'"

John could not continue, for at that point Elvira Rempel burst into tears.

John had actually thought about skipping that section. He'd even discussed doing so with Ruby. But it was the next section in the group's study of the biblical book of James. Like other evangelical Christians, John believed firmly in the Bible, which meant he believed in studying the whole Bible, even sections that were uncomfortable. Besides, Elvira knew what passage they were studying, and she had come anyway, so maybe it was all right. He and Ruby had finally decided to forge ahead and trust God to sort out the situation. Now, watching the usually self-possessed woman weep, he wondered if it had been the right decision.

Ruby and another woman immediately went over to Elvira and held her until gradually the crying subsided. The other group members shuffled uncomfortably in their seats.

"I'm sorry," Elvira managed to say at last. "It's just that it . . . we really don't know what will happen tomorrow, do we? And people really can vanish . . ."

The other members of the group sat silently. They could never remember seeing Elvira cry before, but they all remembered that night just over two months earlier when Jake had been at Bible study with Elvira for the last time. Never a very talkative man, he had been especially quiet that night. After it was over, even though the gathering had ended later than usual, he had taken Elvira home and then told her he had to go into the office to check on some things. He had never been seen again. A couple of days later, his car had been found in a parking lot in the downtown area near the Winnipeg bus terminal, with no evidence of foul play. Jake was a big man, nearly a foot taller than John Smyth and seventy pounds heavier, and he was a dependable, conscientious sort. It was difficult to believe he had just vanished.

"Perhaps it would be good if you talked about it," John prompted gently.

"Yes," she said. "It's time . . ." After a while, she continued. "I'm sorry I haven't talked about it much up to now. It's just been so hard. The police think that he just . . . left, but he wouldn't do that. I know he wouldn't. But they didn't find . . ." More tears. Then she sat up straighter, took an unsteady breath, and told the story from the beginning.

"It wasn't really unusual for Jake to go into work in the evening, but not usually that late. Jake seemed to be in a strange mood all evening. He hardly spoke to me on the way home from Bible study. We came into the house, and he walked all through it. I thought at the time that he was checking to make sure everything was in order, that no one had broken in while we were gone. Now I wonder whether he was . . . saying good-bye."

Elvira sniffed, choked, and seemed to be on the verge of sobbing again but took a deep breath and went on. "You all know Jake was a good man who loved God and tried to do what was right. He treated his customers fairly. What you probably don't know, and Jake never talked about, was that when he was running his trucking company, he paid his workers better than other companies, and he gave them extra benefits, like good disability insurance, that he didn't have to give. He saw himself as a servant—not only to his customers but also to his employees. We lived pretty simply and were still able to give a lot of money away to the church and other charitable causes. But there was a price to be paid. Jake's company didn't make as much money as other companies did, and when the downturn in the economy came, he began to lose money. He was really worried. He was afraid he was going to lose the whole company and all the employees would lose their jobs. When Grant Parkinson came along and suggested a merger with Winnipack, it seemed an answer to prayer. Rempel Trucking became the transportation arm of Winnipack. All the employees kept their jobs, Winnipack got direct control of its transportation system, and Jake became vice president for the trucking division.

"Anyway, the first year or so at Winnipack, Jake was very happy. Everything seemed to be going well, and he didn't have the worry of keeping Rempel Trucking afloat. His sixtieth birthday party last December was a big celebration. Well, you remember that. Most of you were there."

She looked searching around the room, saw the nods and caring looks, bit her lip. Ruby patted her back gently, and she continued.

"But even before that, last fall, some things had started to go badly. It was one thing after another. First, you remember that Jake's mother died in early October. She had been unwell for quite a while, but losing her was still very hard on Jake. Then our Jared moved away, and he was the last of our children still in Manitoba. And Jake's cousin Abe went missing in November—I don't know whether we ever told you about that. And things got unpleasant for Jake at work too, after the birthday party. Just after Christmas, the dispatcher ran off with the wife of one of the drivers Jake had hired. Then Mr. Parkinson's marriage got into trouble. In fact, his wife left him just after Jake disappeared. Those things kind of poisoned the atmosphere at work, and it wasn't as much fun to go in anymore. Plus, Mr. Parkinson wanted to change some of the policies and employee benefits that Jake had put into place, and he didn't like that, even though he knew some things had to change to keep costs under control. None of those things affected Jake directly, but added together . . . well, they made him depressed. He started working longer hours, trying to help fix things. That's what he was doing the night he dropped me off at home and never came back.

"This last part is so hard. I have never told any of you this. After Jake left and I reported him missing to the police, Mr. Parkinson came to see me and told me that over one hundred thousand dollars was missing from the company and that Jake was the only one who'd had access to it. He didn't report this to the police, but I'm afraid Jake took the money and then . . . I don't know, but he wasn't acting anymore like the Jake I had known for thirty-seven years.

"Mr. Parkinson has been very generous. He has continued to pay Jake's salary into our account—it's the kind of thing Jake used to do for employees, and it has been good to see Grant continue that tradition. But it hurts at the same time— that now Jake and I need the kind of help we used to give others. I know Mr. Parkinson can't keep paying the salary forever, and that's all right. I'll get by. But I miss Jake so much."

Elvira lapsed into crying again. When she had again gained control of herself, John Smyth said, "That's a heavy burden. Let's stop and pray right now for Elvira and Jake."

That night, John Smyth lay in bed looking at the ceiling. "I don't think I have ever seen Elvira Rempel cry before," he said.

"I told you, John. She is a very private woman, and she's always been so . . . strong. She and Jake have helped so many people over the years. It must have taken a lot for her to admit she needs help now. She has been carrying all that inside for two months, ever since their kids went back home, and I think she finally had to set it down. She couldn't keep carrying it all alone."

Chapter 8

WEDNESDAY, MAY 26

Rachel, John Smyth's beautiful secretary, stood in his doorway, the morning sun gleaming on her long blonde hair. "There is a woman here to see you," she said. "A Mrs. Rempel."

"Sure. Show her in." John Smyth had an open-door policy. One of the things he liked about his job was that he never knew who was going to drop in to see him unannounced—the pastor of a big church, a missionary from the other end of the world, a teenager trying to get her first article published, an older person bringing in the obituary of a beloved spouse. Or a friend from church whose husband had gone missing . . .

Elvira Rempel showed no trace of last night's weeping. Her face, devoid of makeup as usual, was composed, and she wore a simple dark suit. "Good morning, John," she said.

"Elvira! Come in."

"I hope I'm not disturbing you."

"Not at all. Sit down. Can I get you a cup of coffee?"

"No, thank you." She paused. "John, I have come to ask you a favor."

"Sure. What is it?"

"Could you come to my house and help me clean out Jake's clothes and things and take them to Grace Mission?"

"Elvira, are you sure you want to do that?"

"Yes, John, I have been thinking about it all night, ever since you read that verse about the people vanishing like mist. It was as if God was speaking to my spirit, saying Jake really has vanished and isn't coming back."

Smyth had heard this kind of thing before. Sometimes he was convinced it was God speaking to a person. But sometimes it was just the person's own emotional reaction to something that had happened. "Elvira," he asked again, "are you sure?"

"Yes, John."

"But what if Jake comes back and you have given away all of his clothes?"

"If Jake comes back, it will be as if he has been raised from the dead, and in that case new clothes will be most appropriate. I won't be giving away his personal effects, the things that have good memories, but the rest are just clothes, and they would be better on some poor person's back than hanging in Jake's closet. He would want that. Besides, if Jake comes back and we are too hard up by then to buy new clothes, we can always go down to Grace Mission and get some of his clothes or somebody else's. Jake grew up poor, and it wouldn't be the first time he had to wear secondhand clothes."

John shook his head. "Okay, Elvira, if you want, I'll come help. But I can't come this weekend. I have to go to British Columbia. It will have to wait until next week."

"Couldn't you come this evening?" she pressed. "It won't

take long. Jake didn't have that many clothes, and this is something I feel I should do now. Even if you don't take everything, you could take some things, and we could sort out the rest later."

One of his weaknesses, Smyth reflected, was that he had trouble saying no. Ruby would not be happy that he would be out another night so close to going away for the weekend. If they could find a babysitter, perhaps he would bring her along.

Jake and Elvira's house was in an expensive area south of the Assiniboine River, but it was modest in comparison to its neighbors—a simple two-story, four-bedroom structure that was far less expensive than one would expect for the owner of a trucking company or the vice president of a large company.

Elvira greeted John and Ruby at the door. "Thank you for coming. Would you like some tea before we go upstairs?"

"Thanks, Elvira," Ruby replied, "but I think we should just get started."

"That's what I expected." As she led them upstairs, Elvira explained, "I am really sorry to ask you to do this, but it was something I just didn't think I could handle on my own."

"That's okay," Ruby replied. "We understand."

"I don't think you've ever been in our bedroom," Elvira said, leading them into a large sunny room decorated with photos of children and grandchildren. "Jake's clothes are in the dresser by that wall and at the far end of the closet."

Ruby began opening the dresser drawers and transferring the clothes into the boxes she and John had brought with them. John went to the closet and began taking the clothes off the hangers and laying them out on the bed. Elvira unobtrusively sat down on a chair in the corner of the room and sighed, looking down at the floor. John gently, almost reverently, checked the pockets of the clothes, folded them neatly, and put them into the boxes. When Ruby had finished with the dresser drawers, she helped John with the closet.

Jake Rempel's clothes were neat, clean, and tasteful, but not expensive. The pockets had little in them—some loose change, a paper napkin, a church bulletin, some theater tickets, and a single slightly crumpled photograph in the pocket of one of the suit coats. John walked over and handed the theater tickets and the photo to Elvira.

Tears began to well up in Elvira's eyes. "This must be one of the last photos taken of Jake and me."

John looked at the photo. It showed four couples standing around a table. John recognized Jake and Elvira. He also thought he recognized the couple next to them from pictures he had seen in the newspaper—Grant Parkinson, a handsome, well-dressed man in his fifties, and his wife, Shirley, a good-looking blonde a few years younger.

"Who is this?" he asked, pointing to a younger couple who appeared to be in their twenties. The man was tall, with brown hair, the woman a few inches shorter and blonde.

"That's Mark Driemer, one of the drivers, and his wife, Charlene. Such a beautiful young woman. I don't know why she would leave her husband and run off with that dispatcher person, who was ten years older and not very nice." Pointing to a middle-aged couple, she added, "And this is Al and Cathy Young. Al was one of the drivers who worked for Jake for quite a few years before the merger. He is a good man. I think he is off work now because of a bad back. This was taken in early December, at a Christmas party."

John Smyth thought that something about the photo reminded him of someone he had seen lately, but he couldn't place which one. Perhaps it was Parkinson and his wife, whose pictures had been in the paper.

"There are more clothes in the spare bedroom," Elvira

said suddenly. She led them out into the hall and into the next room. "Jake kept his work clothes in here." She opened the closet door to reveal some flannel shirts, a couple of jackets, work boots and running shoes, and some T-shirts and blue jeans stacked on the shelf. John and Ruby took these clothes out, too, checked the pockets, and put the clothes into a box.

They carried the boxes downstairs, where they added four coats, some gloves and hats from the front hall closet, and a couple more jackets from hooks by the back door. Finished, they looked down at the four boxes of clothes. It wasn't much for a man to leave behind.

Ruby put her arms around Elvira. "I'm so sorry, Elvira," she said. "Are you going to be all right?'

"Yes," Elvira choked. "I think I want to be alone for a while now."

Chapter 9

THURSDAY, MAY 27

North Main Street is a blemish on the face of Winnipeg —a depressing strip of pawnshops, dingy bars, cheap hotels, boarded-up stores, and rescue missions. It is populated by alcoholics, drug addicts, prostitutes, the desperately poor, and the deeply committed. On Thursday, John Smyth pulled his battered station wagon up in front of a dirty brick storefront topped with a weathered wooden sign that proclaimed, in unadorned print, "Grace Mission." *Grace* magazine, he reflected, usually boasted a more attractive font and better layout than that old wooden sign. Taking a large cardboard box from the backseat, he approached the door of the dirty storefront and gave it a couple of sharp kicks. The sound reverberated within, and moments later the door was swung open by a man who was taller, rounder, older, and more animated than John Smyth.

"Good morning, John," he said. "No need to kick the door

down. We get enough of that at night." His face and head were hairless except for a close-cropped fringe.

"Good morning, Harry," John replied. "How's life in the high-rent district?"

"I wouldn't know, but life here is hard." His grin softened the hard words. Harry Collins had been director of Grace Mission for more than thirty years.

"I know," said John. "Maybe this will help a little. Elvira Rempel asked me to go over last night and pack up Jake's clothes. I think she's decided he isn't coming back."

"Mmmm. That's tough. Jake and Elvira are good people. They've donated a lot to the mission over the years."

"Harry?"

"Yeah."

"Could you maybe keep some of the best of the clothes for a while, just in case Jake does come back?"

"Shouldn't be too hard. There isn't a big demand for suits and ties down here."

"Yeah, but there's some work clothes here too, and some good coats."

"Well, bring them into my office, and I'll sort them out later."

Harry's office was a small, cheaply furnished room with no name on the door. John set the box down in the corner. "There's three more boxes in the car," he said.

The two men headed for the outside door. Just as they approached it, it burst open and a skinny, scruffy man rushed between them, pushing them to the side. He was of medium height and dressed in filthy, ragged clothes. There was a wild look in his eye. He began running around the room, between the old tables and chairs where many Main Street residents ate their one good meal a day. "Beware of the twin towers!" he shouted. "The towers never sleep! Never sleep in the shadow of the twin towers! They'll fall on you or they'll suck you up inside and you'll never come back! Benny and Danny went inside and never came back! The towers fell on them! They're lost in the dungeons of Mordor, and the Orcs will cut them up with axes! The two towers are evil and . . ."

The man's tongue and his body had stopped suddenly. As he rounded a table, he had come face-to-face with another man—a thin, quiet man in a long white apron. The new man handed the first a dinner roll. He took it in his hand and stared at it.

John Smyth was standing open-mouthed.

"It's okay, John," Harry said. "That's just Daft Darryl. He rants like that sometimes—brain damage from drinking and drugs, I think. He's probably high now. Ever since nine-one-one, he's been obsessed with the twin towers. Can't tell the difference between New York and Winnipeg—or Mordor, for that matter. He's even taken to hanging around the old cold storage towers, shouting that the airplanes are coming to destroy them. Says it's the judgment of God."

"How does he know Tolkien's *Lord of the Rings*?"

"Yeah, he mixes that in too. Who knows? Maybe he snuck into the downtown theater and saw one of the movies. Maybe he read a lot before the drugs destroyed his mind. Who knows what his life once was? Street people don't talk about the past, what they've lost."

"Who are Benny and Danny?"

"Oh, they're real. Buddies of his, almost as far gone as he is. They often hang around together. It's sad really. He's rather a hopeless case."

"He is *not* hopeless! None of us is!" The quiet man in the apron had spoken suddenly and fiercely. "He understands food and love!"

Daft Darryl was still looking stupidly at the bun. He

looked up and grinned. The other man put his arm around his shoulders.

"You are right, David," Harry Collins said. "John, do you remember David Mackenzie? A year ago, he was also on the street. Now he's one of our most reliable workers. He gives me hope, reminds me that the grace of God really can change people."

John Smyth was lost in thought, meditating on how people change, for good and evil, and how some do not change, continuing on in the course they have chosen for their lives—people like Harry Collins, for instance, who had been serving faithfully in Grace Mission for more than thirty years.

Sergeant Troy Wesson was meditating too. The investigation was making little progress, and he was troubled. This morning he sat in his police car at the chain-up area. Vehicles whizzed past—battered pickup trucks, RVs, beat-up Toyotas, rusty old Buicks, logging trucks, a transport truck with a distinctive orange logo. But Wesson barely registered the traffic. Instead, he was staring up at the wooded hillside. Just to the left of the chain-up area was the driveway up to Gerard Hawkins's cabin and work area, populated with fantastic sculptures carved out of once-living wood. A kilometer closer to town, he knew, was Mary Pendragon's place. He could just see the smoke from her chimney in the distance. In the other direction was Gary and Heather Thompson's place, the farthest of the three from town. He could see no smoke from there.

Suddenly he sat up straighter. Higher up the mountain from Hawkins's place, and closer to town, he could see another thin column of smoke rising into the sky.

Wesson got out of the car, locked it, and started walking up the mountain through the trees. Whatever the source of the smoke, it was obvious that no driveway led to it. Wesson enjoyed the outdoors and was in good condition, but the climbing was hard, through bushes and around boulders and trees. He did his best to move silently and to keep a straight course, although he could no longer see the smoke once he started through the trees. After ten or fifteen minutes, he caught a glimpse of what must be Gerard Hawkins's house, away to the side. He slowed his pace. He still could not see the smoke or hear anything but the sounds of the forest.

Suddenly, as he continued to push his way forward, he stepped into a gap in the undergrowth and realized it was a path—narrow, twisting, and not entirely free of vegetation, but a discernible path nonetheless. It seemed to angle down toward Hawkins's clearing in one direction and farther up the mountain in the other. The path made it easier to move quietly.

After another five or ten minutes, Wesson reached his goal. It was so small and blended so well into the forest that he almost blundered into it, in spite of his caution. He pulled back slightly behind some bushes.

In front of him was a hut composed of rough slabs of tree trunk, leaning together to form a tunnel about ten feet long. The slabs seemed to have been rough cut with a chainsaw and were stacked three or four layers deep to form a reasonable barrier to cold and rain. Over the whole was draped a dingy gray tarp, and another piece of canvas hung down over the front as a sort of door. A small pipe protruding from the far end emitted a thin, steady stream of gray smoke. Only a couple of feet of trampled earth separated the structure from the surrounding undergrowth. The structure blended into the surrounding vegetation so well that it almost seemed to have grown there naturally.

Wesson stood looking at the hut for a couple of minutes. He half expected a dwarf or an elf to emerge from it. Silently, he moved forward, grasped the bottom of the end tarp, flung it back. The dwarf inside sat cross-legged on the floor, shrinking back in fright from Wesson's sudden intrusion. Very pale, with a prominent Gallic nose, he wore a long brown coat over dark pants; he had a black toque on his head, a bushy gray beard, and long, tangled hair. But he wasn't really a dwarf, Wesson realized. He was at least five foot ten, perhaps six feet tall.

They stared at each other in fear and wonder for several minutes. As Wesson's eyes adjusted to the dark interior, he discovered it was less primitive than he had expected. Logs had been placed at intervals across the hut and more wood slabs laid across them to form a serviceable wooden floor. Rainwater running down the mountainside would flow between the logs, leaving the occupant dry on the floor above. In the back corner, on a bed of flat stones, was a small wood stove, and beside it was a mattress covered with thick comforters and a sleeping bag. In the front area were some metal storage canisters, a wooden box that served as a rude chair or table, some cooking pots, a lantern, an ax, two hunting rifles, and a chainsaw.

"What do you want?" growled the inhabitant. "Do you have a search warrant?"

The question, in such a setting, was so ludicrous that Wesson burst into laughter. He held out his hand. "I'm Sergeant Troy Wesson," he said, "from Prince Rupert."

"I'm Isaac." The man did not take Wesson's hand.

"You live here?"

The other man nodded.

"How long?"

"A long time."

"You live alone?"

"No. My wife and three kids are upstairs."

Wesson would have laughed, but the man's eyes were serious and wild at the same time, without a trace of humor. It

94

almost seemed as if he believed what he said, as if he expected a wife and children to come running down nonexistent stairs at any moment. "How do you live?" he asked. "What do you eat?"

"What lives and grows in the forest."

Wesson wasn't sure if it was the answer to his question or another question. He was becoming convinced that the man was mentally unbalanced. Whether he had been so before he moved into the forest or he had become so as a result of living there, Wesson couldn't say. "Do you need anything?" he asked.

"No," the other replied after a moment.

The conversation was going nowhere. Wesson wasn't sure it would get any better, but he decided to try anyway. "You know the chain-up area down below?"

The man nodded.

"Have you seen anything suspicious happening down there?"

The man seemed puzzled but shook his head.

Wesson pulled two of the reconstruction drawings from his pocket and unfolded them. "Have you ever seen either of these two people?" he asked, handing the pictures to the man, who stared at them dumbly. "The man is in his thirties, about five foot nine. The woman is in her midtwenties, about five foot seven, with shoulder-length blonde hair. We found their bodies down below the chain-up area a few days ago. They had been murdered and their bodies cut up with a chainsaw."

The man shuddered, and the wild look returned to his eyes.

Wesson continued, "They were probably killed several months ago. Did you see or hear anything down at the chain-up area?"

The man shook his head. "I did not see them."

"Did you hear anything? A chainsaw?"

"I heard Hawk's chainsaw."

Wesson didn't know whether he was more shocked that the man seemed to be implicating Hawkins or that he knew Hawkins's name. "Where? Down at the chain-up area?"

"I hear it all the time."

Even now, if he strained his ears, Wesson could hear a distant whine that was surely Hawkins at work with his chainsaw. "Did you ever hear his chainsaw down at the chain-up area?"

"Hawk is a very troubled man, with his wife," the other said.

"Mr. Hawkins has a wife?"

"She is upstairs too," the man said pointing upward. "That is why he is troubled. He is a troubled man. We are all troubled men."

"Have you ever seen Hawkins's wife?"

The man looked away slyly. Wesson did not expect him to speak, but he did. "No. She was always upstairs."

"Did Hawkins kill her?"

"No."

"Did Hawkins cut her up?"

"No. That would be crazy."

"Did you ever hear Hawkins's chainsaw down at the chain-up area?" Wesson repeated.

The man's eyes widened and grew wilder. "Man is born to trouble as surely as sparks fly upward."

Wesson did not know what to make of this. "Do you ever talk to Hawkins?"

The man nodded.

"How often?"

The man shrugged.

Wesson had another thought. "Do you ever talk to Mary Pendragon?"

"No!" the other screamed so loudly that Wesson nearly fell backward from his squatting position. "She is an evil woman! Flee the evil woman!"

Wesson remembered that he had seen no path leading from Isaac's hut toward Mary Pendragon's house. "Why do you say she is an evil woman?"

"She is a black-hearted witch! She does evil things in the dark."

"What evil things? Does she kill people?"

"Maybe. Witches do."

"Did she kill these two people?" Wesson asked, pointing to the pictures.

"Maybe. I don't know."

"Did Hawkins kill them?"

"He carves people sometimes."

"He carves people? You mean with his chainsaw?"

"Yes, he carves wooden people."

"But not real people?"

"I don't know. Maybe they're real."

Wesson felt as if he was talking to someone from a foreign country who was using English words but had no idea what he was saying. "Thank you, Isaac. Perhaps I will come and see you again. If you ever have anything to tell me or if you need any help, can you ask Mr. Hawkins to phone me?"

Isaac nodded.

Wesson crawled out of the hut and stood up, stretching his back. He stood for a minute pondering his next step, then started down the trail toward Hawkins's place. Coming down the trail from above, he could see the whole layout of the clearing—the log cabin, Hawkins's truck, and the large work space under the canopy. Hawkins was hunched over a log with his chainsaw, sending chips flying in a broad arc, a picture of total concentration. Wesson watched him for a while. The man was definitely skilled with a chainsaw. Wesson shuddered at the implications of his thought. He walked around the clearing so that he would come into Hawkins's vision from the front. He waited until Hawkins paused and stood back for a moment, then called out, "Mr. Hawkins!"

Hawkins straightened and stood back farther, letting the saw whine to a stop. He glared at Wesson.

"Mr. Hawkins, I was wondering if you had thought of anything else or if there is anything you want to tell me."

Hawkins stood still and said nothing. He shook his head slightly.

Wesson moved closer. "I have just been talking to Isaac," he said. "You didn't tell me about Isaac."

"How did you find him?"

"I saw the smoke from his stove."

Hawkins nodded. "He's an old man who just wants be left alone. Why don't you leave him alone?"

"Since he lives in the area, he might know something about the murders. He might have seen something."

"He can't see anything from his hut. There are too many trees."

"Mr. Hawkins, do you think he could have killed the people at the chain-up area?"

Hawkins was silent for a moment. "No," he said, "he wouldn't kill anyone."

"How do you know?"

"He just couldn't."

"How do you know that? Because you committed the murders yourself?"

"I could—but I didn't."

"How does Isaac live?"

"He hunts, fishes, collects berries."

"Does he scavenge down at the chain-up area?"

Hawkins stood stock-still. "I give him food sometimes, even took him into town a couple of times."

"Why, Mr. Hawkins?"

"He needed help. I gave him food. He's a harmless old man. You won't take him away from there, will you?"

"I don't think so, no."

"He's a harmless old man, living safely in the woods. Leave him alone."

"What happened to your wife, Mr. Hawkins?"

In a flash, Hawkins had flung down the saw in Wesson's general direction, turned, and run full speed into the woods. Startled into immobility for a few seconds, Wesson quickly recovered himself and went off after him. If he had thought for a moment, he would have realized what a crazy thing it was he was doing, running off alone into endless woods chasing a skilled woodsman. No one knew where he was, and he was armed with only his police revolver. If Hawkins got the upper hand on him, a likely scenario because Hawkins was a big, powerful man, his body might never be found—except perhaps in pieces down by the chain-up area.

Hawkins ran haphazardly through the woods, following no trail but heading generally up the mountain, away from the road, and away from Isaac's hut. Wesson could hear him breaking through the brush ahead of him. Wesson followed as fast as he could under the circumstances. Tree branches pummeled his face and arms, leaving scratches and bruises. His feet stumbled over roots and rocks. Twice he fell headlong, driving the wind from his lungs. Once he almost dashed his head against a large rock. He lost his hat somewhere. He knew he was losing ground to the bigger man ahead.

He became aware that he could no longer hear the pounding of feet, the breaking of tree branches. He slowed, gasping for breath. More warily, he moved forward along the broken trail Hawkins had left through the brush. Every few steps, he turned quickly and looked all around. If Hawkins was circling around behind him, he would be an easy target.

He was still moving forward when his ears caught an unexpected sound ahead and to the right, through a thicket of trees. Approaching as quietly as he could, Wesson caught a glimpse of red flannel. Hawkins leaned against a tree, shoulders heaving under the plaid shirt. He was groaning, a most unearthly sound. Wesson stood mesmerized at the edge of the thicket. He waited until gradually the moaning subsided.

"Mr. Hawkins."

Hawkins turned slowly. Blood and sweat ran down his face—and tears. "My wife is dead," he said. "Go away and leave me alone!"

"Did you kill her?"

"No! She died—not here. Go away."

He began to moan once more and turned away.

Wesson turned and retraced his steps down through the broken branches, eventually retrieving his hat, which had a small tear in it.

Back at the police station in Prince Rupert, Wesson phoned Len Archbold at home.

"Gee, Boss, don't you believe in letting me have a day off?"

Wesson ignored the complaint. "Archie, when you come in tomorrow, I want you to check up on the history of Gerard Hawkins. He may have moved up here a few years ago from Cariboo country, so talk to the office in Williams Lake. He had a wife—find out what happened to her."

"You're thinking maybe he's our guy and he's killed before?"

"I don't know. That's what we need to find out. You also missed one of the residents living by the chain-up area."

"Nooo. Who?"

"An old hermit named Isaac, lives in a lean-to up behind Hawkins's place."

"How'd you find him?"

"Saw smoke from a little stove he has."

"Well, we said the mountains are filled with hermits and weirdos who don't show up in the records. Is he a suspect?"

"Could be. He has a chainsaw, and he seems to be playing Russian roulette with all the chambers empty."

There was a pause. "Oh. You mean he's a nutcase."

"Seriously mentally ill would be my guess."

"Does he hang around the chain-up area?"

"Maybe. He seems pretty destitute. I wouldn't be surprised if he spends a fair amount of time down there scrounging from the trash barrel or begging for handouts from passing truckers."

"You figure the two victims caught him stealing and he killed them?"

"Could be."

"Did you bring him in?"

"On what? Suspicion?"

"Bring him in on a mental-health warrant."

"What if he's just crazy but innocent? If I bring him in, they'll treat him in Vancouver for a month and then release him into the downtown east side. He'd be dead in a couple of weeks. They're not going to fix him anyway. He's happy in the woods, and I don't think he's going anywhere. I'm just going to leave him alone for now."

"Yeah," said Archbold, "I'd rather be in the woods than Vancouver any day. Grizzlies are safer company than some of what they've got down there."

Chapter 10

FRIDAY, MAY 28

Wesson did not know if it was true that a murderer always returns to the scene of the crime. He did know that he himself felt irresistibly drawn to the chain-up area, like a moth to a flame that would destroy it. The attraction felt like a deadly fascination with evil. He told himself that it couldn't be that, that perhaps the draw was his instinct telling him the solution was to be found in the vicinity of the chain-up area if only he could see it. He told himself he was just determined to keep poking under every rock until he found the truth.

If he had talked to his practical-minded wife, Sandy, about it, he suspected she would say he was becoming obsessed with the case, taking it far too personally. She would also suggest once more that he take Sundays off and go to church with her. He had no intentions of discussing the case with Sandy.

He had managed to resist the pull of the chain-up area

until after noon today, but one fifteen found him rolling east along the highway. About five kilometers before the chain-up area, he saw a battered red Toyota pickup parked at an odd angle at the side of the road. In fall, it was not uncommon to see such vehicles pulled off the road in odd places and parked at odd angles—left in a hurry by hunters pursuing hunches through the trees and underbrush. But this was not hunting season. It was also not berry-picking season. Wesson pulled in behind the red truck. There was no one in it and no one around it. Before moving on, he tried to call up the license plate number on his car computer but couldn't connect, a common occurrence in the mountains. He radioed in to Mildred.

"I'm sorry, Sergeant, the main computer is down. I'll have it checked when it comes back up and get back to you."

"Thanks, Mildred."

Wesson had intended to go past the chain-up area and head straight for Gerard Hawkins's place, but catching a glimpse of something white in the chain-up area, he decided to pull in. It was a recent-model Honda. Pulling in beside it, he saw a short, bald man with a reddish beard and wire-rimmed glasses walking around the chain-up area, pausing from time to time to stretch.

Wesson got out of his car and approached the little man— who on closer inspection was very little indeed. Couldn't have been much taller than Sandy, who was one-point-five-three meters—five foot one. "Good afternoon," Wesson said.

"Hello," the little man replied.

"I am Sergeant Wesson of the RCMP. Can I ask who you are?"

"Sure. My name is John Smyth." Seeing a familiar expression in the Sergeant's eyes, the little man sighed in resignation, pulled out his wallet, and handed over his driver's license. "I really am John Smyth."

"Okay. But you don't spell it the usual way."

"No. There is probably some historical reason why my family spells it that way. It's not that uncommon, actually—" Smyth stopped talking. He could tell that Wesson didn't really care.

"You're from Winnipeg?"

"Yes."

"What brings you out this way?"

"I'm editor of *Grace* magazine, which is published in Winnipeg. I flew out to Prince George last night and rented the car this morning. I'm on my way to Prince Rupert to research a story."

"A story on the murders?"

"Murders? Oh, you mean the chainsaw murders? No, I—"

"Then why did you stop here?"

"Just to stretch my—wait, this is the place, isn't it? Where the cut-up bodies were found?"

"Yes, in the woods just over there."

"Wow! And I have been walking around here all alone. Ruby won't like that."

"Who's Ruby?"

"My wife. I told her I would be careful. It's a long story."

"If you didn't know this was the place, why did you stop here?"

"Just by accident."

"You had an accident?"

"No, I just happened to stop here to take a break. It's a long drive from Prince George to Prince Rupert."

"If you came here to write the story, you would have known this was the place."

"But I didn't come to write that story. *Grace* is a church

magazine. I came to write a story about the revival in the Grace Evangelical Church in Prince Rupert."

"What revival? What's a revival?"

"A revival is a significant increase in church attendance and Christian commitment. It started a couple of years ago with an Alcoholics Victorious program. Well, actually it began before that, when the pastor decided to go out into the woods one day every week and pray. Then they started the Alcoholics Victorious program—that's a program to help alcoholics overcome their addiction, but it's more specifically Christian than Alcoholics Anonymous. Anyway, some people came to Christ—uh, became Christians—as a result of the course, and that got some other people interested in the church. Anyway, in the last year, attendance at the church has gone up by about fifty people, and twenty-seven people have been baptized . . . as new Christians. That's quite remarkable for a small church in a small town."

Wesson was dumbfounded. He knew his wife was now going to church, but he hadn't known anything about this. How could he not know about something that was going on in his own town when this stranger from Winnipeg apparently did? He sighed. "So you didn't come to write about the murders, and you don't want pictures of the two victims?"

"Well, now that you mention it, the murders might make an interesting sidebar to the church story."

Wesson went over to his car and pulled two pictures out of a large brown envelope. He handed them to Smyth. "Do you recognize them?"

Smyth looked at the pictures. "No," he said slowly.

"Well, welcome to the Prince Rupert area, Mr. Smyth. I hope you enjoy your visit."

"Thank you. Have you ever been to a service at Grace Evangelical Church in Prince Rupert, Sergeant?"

"No," Wesson said shortly. Then, as if to explain, he added, "No offense, but I don't really have time for that. I have some murders to solve. I'm dealing with matters of life-and-death."

"So is the church," Smyth replied.

As the white car pulled out of the parking lot in the direction of Prince Rupert, Wesson called in to the office. "Mildred, there's another license plate number I would like you to check, a B.C. plate, PKR 330."

A few minutes later, driving up the long lane to Hawkins's place, Wesson found himself listening intently. He wasn't sure what he was hearing. Then it struck him. It wasn't what he was hearing but what he wasn't hearing. There was no characteristic whine of a chainsaw as he approached Hawkins's place. He thought he might have heard it earlier from the chain-up area but wasn't sure.

The large clearing under the tarpaulin canopy was heavily populated, but all of the inhabitants were wooden. Wesson approached the house and knocked on the door. "Mr. Hawkins!" he called. There was no answer. He knocked again. No answer. He turned from the door and called again. He noted that Hawkins's truck was in the driveway, but there was still no answer.

Wesson breathed out sharply and looked around, then headed toward the west end of the property and the narrow path to Isaac's hut. It was a good fifteen-minute hike, but certainly easier than Wesson's first climb to the hut. He tried to approach it unobserved, but Isaac was sitting cross-legged in the doorway reading a book.

There was no point in being cautious now. "Good morning, Isaac," Wesson said.

Isaac nodded but said nothing.

"How are you today?"

"Okay."

"Have you seen Mr. Hawkins today?" Wesson looked around the clearing as he asked it, but there was no sign of anyone else.

"No."

"Have you heard him working with his chainsaw today?"

"I don't remember."

"Are you getting enough to eat?" The old man was dressed in the same bulky outfit as the day before, but in the brighter light Wesson could see that his face and hands were very thin.

"G—" the man started, then tried another tack: "The woods supply me well."

"What are you reading?"

"See this pretty bookmark," the man replied, holding it up. "Hawk's woman gave it to—"

His answer was interrupted by a piercing, haunting shriek. Wesson suspected the startled terror he saw in the old man's eyes might be mirroring his own. "Mary Pendragon?" he asked.

The old man shrugged but nodded slightly.

The cry came again, undulating this time, almost as if the shriek contained words. Wesson began to move toward the sound. Breaking through a place where the undergrowth was least dense, Wesson found himself following not a path but a way through the woods nonetheless. The way angled west and down along the mountainside in the direction of Mary Pendragon's cabin and the shriek. He had to pick his way carefully so as not to lose the track, and it took him even longer to reach Mary Pendragon's place than it had to reach Isaac's. Periodically he would hear the shrieking again, and as he got closer, he realized it was sometimes interspersed with a lower chanting.

Catching a glimpse of a black roof through the trees, he

slowed down. Moving carefully around a rock outcrop, he suddenly found himself on the lip of a horseshoe-shaped depression, about ten feet deep, ten feet long, and six feet across. Three candles flickered at the rounded inner end of the depression. A figure in black bowed before the candles. An eerie keening sound assailed Wesson's ears—part chant, part moan, and part howl. The sound was then joined by a strange whirring. Seven tiny figurines leaned against the rock wall before the kneeling black creature. As the creature straightened, Wesson caught a flash of silvery light. An elongated limb reached out toward the seven tiny figurines. Wesson heard the whirring again, and the arm of one of the figurines suddenly flew off into the air, then the other arm, its head and, one by one, the legs. Then the arm of a second figurine flew up.

The black-clad creature whirled unexpectedly, pointed the whirring limb up toward Wesson, and shrieked, "What are you doing here?! Curses fall on you! How dare you intrude?!"

Wesson, towering above the black figure of Mary Pendragon, had the distinct impression that it was she who was towering over him. Summoning his strength, he asked, "What are you doing? Did you kill the people down by the chain-up area?" He had meant to use his forceful policeman's voice, but his voice came out weak, almost in a whisper.

"I've touched no one," she snarled. "I need touch no one. The spirits touch people, and the people do their bidding. You can't touch me. Now, be gone!"

Wesson really had no reason to be there. He could think of no questions to ask. But he did not recall deciding to leave, just found himself sliding backward through the trees away from Mary Pendragon. Halfway back toward Isaac's cabin, his hands began to shake. He sat for a few minutes on a rock until his mind gradually cleared.

When he reached the clearing, he could not see Isaac. He lifted the tarp and peered into the hut, but Isaac was not there either. He called, "Isaac! Isaac!" but there was no answer.

He moved on to Hawkins's cabin, but there was no one there either. He scouted around the east side of the property, wondering if there might be other paths, and found what he was looking for. A path led down and to the east, winding with the slope of the land and ending at the Thompsons' house. Gary's logging truck was gone, but the dirty pickup stood in the driveway.

Wesson approached the house warily. After his knock, it was half a minute before the curtains in the front window rustled and a voice asked through the door, "Who is it?"

"Sergeant Wesson, Mrs. Thompson. May I talk with you for a minute?"

After another short delay, the door swung open, and Heather Thompson stood in the doorway. She wore a long-sleeved knit dress.

"Mrs. Thompson, I am looking for Mr. Hawkins. Do you know where he might be?"

"Hawkins? You mean the man who lives down the road—the wood carver?"

"Yes. Is he here?"

"No. I haven't seen him. He never comes here."

"Oh." Wesson paused. "How are you doing?"

"We're fine."

"Mrs. Thompson, could I trouble you for a glass of water?"

Heather turned, letting the screen door shut behind her and leaving Wesson standing on the doorstep. She returned a few moments later with a glass. Wesson drank, handed the glass back to her, and said, "Thank you." He had been tramping around in the woods for over an hour, and he could feel the sweat running down his back.

"How did you get here?" she asked, as if she had just noticed his police car was not parked in the driveway.

"I walked over along the path from Mr. Hawkins's place." He turned to go. "You will let me know if you need any help or anything, won't you?"

She nodded. He turned and began the walk back to Hawkins's place. Going back was harder than coming. It was uphill, and he was tired from tramping through the brush.

Hawkins's clearing seemed as deserted as before. Wesson knocked on the door of the cabin and called, but no one appeared. He felt like a thoughtless guest who had come so often that people were now avoiding him.

Strolling back to the car, he once again looked over Hawkins's magnificent carvings. The eagles, the bear cubs climbing a tree trunk, and the hunter were still there. The small bear standing on its hind legs was nearing completion. The standing bear with the mutilated paw had been shoved to a back corner of the work area. Wesson winced when he saw that. One of the pieces that had been unformed before had been transformed into an eagle tearing a salmon on a tree limb, delicate and magnificent. That reminded Wesson of the magnificent bear that he had supposed was eating a salmon on a log. That one had been in the center of the work area. Whatever was there now had been covered with a blue tarpaulin.

Wesson went over, pulled back the tarpaulin, and gasped. There was the bear, as magnificent as ever, but the unformed log it was standing on had been transformed into a man, his eyes wide with terror and his mouth open in a scream. What Wesson had assumed was a salmon in the bear's mouth was the man's mangled arm, thrown up in a fruitless effort of defense.

"Now what," Wesson asked himself, "is the significance of that?"

Reaching the end of Hawkins's driveway, Wesson caught a glimpse of something shiny—a transport truck parked in the chain-up area. Pulling in beside the vehicle, he considered that in that fantastic afternoon he had already encountered a dwarf (John Smyth), a wood nymph (Isaac), a witch (Mary Pendragon), and a magician with a disappearing act (Gerard Hawkins). He wondered what he would encounter next.

No driver was at the wheel of the truck, and he thought for a moment that it might have been abandoned. He was about to radio in the license plate number when a short, burly, red-haired man came out of the woods, straightening his fly and heading toward the truck. Wesson got out of his car and approached him.

"It's a long way from Prince George to Prince Rupert," the man grinned.

Wesson smiled back. "Good morning. Can I see your license?"

The man pulled his wallet from his pocket and handed over the document. The man's name was George Schmidt.

"Thank you, Mr. Schmidt. What are you hauling?"

Instead of answering, the man walked over to the truck and pulled some documents from the passenger seat. Handing them over, he said, "General merchandise for a department store in Rupert."

Handing them back, Wesson said, "Thank you, Mr. Schmidt. You drive this route very often?"

"Couple of times a month."

"Do you stop at this chain-up area often?"

"Sometimes. Depends on how much coffee I drink, how the load's riding, weather conditions."

"Do you know what was found here a few days ago, Mr. Schmidt?"

"No. What?"

"Don't you read the newspapers, Mr. Schmidt, listen to the news?"

"I don't read the papers much, and radio reception's not good in the mountains. The reason I like driving is that it's away from everything else. I don't have to worry about all the junk that's going on."

"Wait here a moment, Mr. Schmidt." Wesson went over to his car and pulled an envelope out of the front seat. Pulling two photographs out of the envelope and handing them to the truck driver, he asked, "Have you seen either of these people around here? The man's about five foot nine, in his thirties. The woman's about five foot seven, blonde, midtwenties."

"No, don't recall seeing them. Are they missing?"

"We found their bodies down in the bush here."

"The chainsaw bodies? I remember some other truckers saying something about that. That was here?"

"Yes, it was here. You sometimes stop here and go into the woods apparently. Did you ever see anything suspicious maybe a few months ago—hear a chainsaw, perhaps?"

"No, I don't remember seeing anything unusual. There are people parked here sometimes, but I don't pay much attention."

Wesson handed him a card. "If you remember anything specific, if you see anything in the future, or if you hear anything from any of the other drivers, even if it doesn't seem that significant, will you get in touch with me?"

"Sure." There was a pause. "Can I go now?"

"Sure." Wesson watched as the burly little man climbed into the big rig, settled himself in the seat, started the big engine, and pulled out onto the highway heading for Prince Rupert.

Before pulling out onto the highway himself, Wesson called in to the office. "Mildred, there's one more license plate number I would like you to check."

"Sure. The computer is up now."

"Oh, okay. I can check it myself."

"I did check on the numbers you gave me before."

"Yeah?"

"The second is a red Honda registered to a car rental agency in Prince George."

"Okay."

"The first is registered to a Charles Haquapar of Prince Rupert."

"What? The doctor?"

"I think so."

"I'm coming back in. Ask Archbold, Leblanc, and Johnson to meet me there in an hour."

"Constable Johnson's not on duty today."

"Okay. Just the other two will do."

Before leaving, Wesson punched some numbers into his in-car computer. The computer told him that the plate was for a transport truck registered to a George Schmidt, an owner-operator working with Long Run Trucking Company, based in Calgary.

Archbold and Leblanc were sitting in the reception area of the police station talking to Mildred when Wesson walked in. The conversation stopped abruptly, and the two followed Wesson into the tiny private office.

"What's up, Boss?" Archbold asked.

"Nothing special. I just wanted to check signals on how the investigation is going. You guys find out anything?"

Archbold said, "I've been doing the house-to-house out on the highway. Nobody seems to have seen anything, and everybody has a chainsaw. I got all the way to the outskirts of Terrace, and I don't think there is much point in going farther toward Prince George."

"No, that's far enough," Wesson said. "Leblanc, what's happening with the missing-persons angle?"

"Gracie Levasseur is still missing. DNA samples have been sent to the lab in Vancouver to check for a match with the dead woman, but the results won't be ready for a while. There are some other missing persons they are also checking, but there's no reason to connect any of them with the Prince Rupert area."

"What's Gracie Levasseur's background?"

"Pretty mundane. She comes from a normal family living in North Bay, Ontario. She didn't get along with her mother and didn't know what to do with herself after high school, so she took off on a trip across country with a boyfriend on a motorcycle. They had an argument, and she split with the boyfriend after about six weeks but just kept going. There is some evidence she worked as a waitress from time to time. The family would hear from her every few months or so, but they haven't heard anything since before Christmas. The girl is of age and hasn't committed any crimes, so she can do what she likes. We're not officially looking for her."

"What about Luther Malone and Amber Long?"

"They are not officially missing either, so no police have been actively looking for them. I am still trying to check their backgrounds. We know Amber Long is from Calgary, but that's about all we know so far. Malone is supposedly from California, but I am not even sure where in California."

"Okay," Wesson said. "Keep checking."

"What about you, Boss?" Archbold asked. "You went back to the chain-up area today, right? Did you find out anything new?"

"Not a lot. On the way out there, I saw Charles Haquapar's pickup parked beside the highway about thirty clicks out."

"The doctor?"

"Yeah. No sign of him, though. When I came back, the truck was gone."

"What was he doing out there—illegal hunting?"

"Who knows? Taking a walk? It is not illegal to park your truck beside the highway and take a walk. Maybe he was visiting a patient."

"Or disposing of one."

Wesson was not sure if Archbold was kidding. Haquapar had a mixed reputation. "Maybe. I doubt it, though."

"Are you going to follow it up?"

Wesson reflected. "I'm not sure. Maybe. I also saw a remarkable carving by Gerard Hawkins—a bear eating a man."

"Do you think maybe he's training bears to cut up people with chainsaws?"

"No, this bear was just using his teeth."

Archbold grimaced.

"I also learned there are paths through the woods between the places of all those people up there—Hawkins, the Thompsons, Mary Pendragon, and the hermit."

"What hermit?" Leblanc wanted to know.

"Oh yeah, I told Archie and put a report in the file. The other day, I found an old man living in a hut up the mountainside between Hawkins's place and Mary Pendragon's. He's a bit off, but as far as I can tell he's harmless."

"Anything else interesting out there?" Archbold wanted to know.

Wesson hesitated. "I also saw Mary Pendragon in a kind of shrine she has out behind her place cutting up dolls with a battery-powered carving knife."

"That sounds pretty suspicious."

"Yeah, but she's weird anyway—fancies herself a witch, I think. But cutting up dolls with a carving knife isn't the same as cutting up real people with a chainsaw. Every time I go out there, I end up with more questions, but I'm not finding many answers. Everybody in the area seems suspicious, but I don't have any hard evidence against anybody. Anyway, starting Monday, Pierre, I want you and Lynn to set up a roadblock out on the highway and question everybody, especially truckers. A lot of them use that highway all the time. Something happened at the chain-up area, and somebody must have seen something."

"A roadblock?" Leblanc smirked. "That will be popular. It'll back up traffic pretty good."

"Yeah," Wesson responded. "Take Rumple along to speed up the process. Archie can handle any calls that come back on your missing-persons angle."

"Do you want us to stop traffic going both ways?"

"Just stop the traffic going out for now. There's only one highway, so no point in stopping the same people coming and going. Take copies of the pictures to show people and to give out whenever you think it useful. You could actually set the roadblock up at the chain-up area. There's good visibility coming up to there, and you can divert all the traffic into the chain-up area to slow them down. There's also plenty of places to park if you want to talk to somebody longer."

"We should keep it quiet that we're planning this?"

"Not necessarily. We're not expecting to catch the killer in the roadblock, just someone who might have seen the killer."

Chapter 11

Sandy Wesson had just put the children's breakfast on the table when Troy walked through the kitchen door. She stared at him open-mouthed. He was wearing a white shirt and tie.

"Thought I'd come to church with you if you don't mind," he said awkwardly.

She swallowed. "No, I don't mind."

Grace Evangelical Church in Prince Rupert was an unpretentious building located on a side street. No steeple, just dark brown wooden siding and a sign in front giving service times. Seeing that the small parking lot was already full, Wesson parked his 4 x 4 on the street. It had taken a little while to get six-year-old John and four-year-old Michelle ready, and the service was just starting when they walked in the door and sat down in a rear pew—the only pew that seemed to have enough space left.

Wesson had not been in this church before. In fact, he had not been in *any* church since he was a young boy. He and Sandy had been married by a justice of the peace. Now he looked around curiously at a place that didn't much resemble—or sound like—the hushed houses of worship he remembered.

The small building seemed full to capacity, with more than two hundred people there—some sitting on extra chairs at the front and back and along one side. The crowd seemed to be largely composed of young families, including a fair sprinkling of Natives, not the white-haired old ladies he remembered from the church of his childhood. Wesson noted uncomfortably that he was one of the few people wearing a tie. On the stage at the front of the church was a band composed of a drummer, a keyboard player, three guitarists (one was playing a bass guitar), and two young women singers. What they were playing was evidently the introduction to a song, because it quickly morphed into a crescendo.

The crowd got to its feet and began clapping and singing to the music. After a few moments, Wesson realized the words to the song had been projected onto a screen at the front of the church. They stood and sang for twenty-five minutes. The rock beat and some of the lyrics reminded Wesson of songs played on the radio five or ten years ago.

Finally, the music ended, the crowd sat down, and a clean-shaven man with brown hair bounded onto the stage.

"That's Pastor Paul," Sandy whispered.

"Good morning! I'm Pastor Paul," the man boomed. Wesson guessed the man must have a portable microphone on his shirt. He also noted that the pastor wore a sports shirt and no tie.

"Welcome to G.E. Church!" Pastor Paul shouted. "We're here to turn on the light!" The crowd groaned, laughed, and applauded.

"I especially want to welcome all of our visitors today. We'd appreciate it if you'd fill out a visitor card in the pew in front of you and put it in the offering plate." Wesson saw the cards marked "visitor" in the rack in front of him but did not touch them.

"We'd also like to welcome a special guest this morning— John Smyth from Winnipeg. He's editor of *Grace* magazine, which all of you members of the church should be getting regularly in the mail. He's come all the way from Winnipeg to write a story about our church. We don't often have representatives from Grace Evangelical Church headquarters visit us, so it's good to have you here. Stand up, John!" Smyth was already standing. The crowd applauded, laughed, and applauded again. Wesson recognized the diminutive editor from their encounter at the chain-up area.

Pastor Paul made a couple of announcements, prayed a short prayer, and said that the offering would be taken. Four people came forward and began passing wooden offering plates along the rows. Before they were finished, the band began playing again. The crowd straggled to its feet and sang for another ten minutes—just two songs this time, but they repeated the second song five times.

The band members laid down their instruments and microphones and sat down among the audience. Pastor Paul bounded back onto the stage and told an Internet joke about whether computers are male or female. Then he prayed briefly, opened the big Bible he had in his hand, and read a story about an army—some Old Testament prophet and a servant seeing an army of fire.

Wesson didn't hear a great deal of the sermon that followed. He was having trouble concentrating. His children, not used to having their father in church, were fidgeting and arguing about which one of them should get to sit next to him.

He finally solved that problem by putting one on each side of him and putting an arm around each of them.

"We often look at things from the wrong perspective," Pastor Paul was saying. "We are blinded by the familiar. If we live on the beach and someone says 'ball,' we may think of a beach ball when what the other person was really talking about is a high-society dance. We don't see God because we are looking for the physical when God is very plainly, but spiritually, there in front of our face."

The pastor spoke passionately and energetically for thirty-five minutes—Wesson checked his watch—and then ended with a prayer. The band played again, and the crowd began to sing. Wesson suddenly noted that at least five people from the crowd had gone forward and were kneeling in front of the stage. Pastor Paul and some other people went and knelt beside them, putting arms over their shoulders. Wesson also thought he saw two teenaged girls dancing arm in arm in the side aisle. After about five minutes, Pastor Paul stood up and boomed, "Thanks for coming. Go with Jesus this week!"

Rather than leaving, the people in the crowd began to shake hands, give hugs, and talk to one another. Several came over and talked to Sandy. Wesson felt a hand on his shoulder. "Welcome here. I'm Paul Postos." Wesson noticed that the man's voice boomed even when he wasn't using a microphone. "You must be Sandy's husband, Troy."

"Yes," Wesson said. "How did you know my name?"

"Oh, Sandy's mentioned you. You're RCMP, right?"

"That's right. Look, Pastor, could I talk to you about something sometime?"

"Sure. Why don't you come back to the church—say, around two thirty this afternoon?"

"Thanks. I'd appreciate that." Wesson had heard Sandy

gasp when he had asked to see the pastor, and as he turned, he saw her brushing her eye with her hand.

Now what's that all about? he wondered.

At two thirty, the church parking lot was virtually empty. Wesson tried the main door to the church, found it unlocked, and went in. The lights were off, but sunlight was streaming in through the mottled-glass windows. Pastor Paul and John Smyth sat sprawled on adjacent pews, talking.

Seeing Wesson, the pastor jumped to his feet. "Come in, come in," he said.

"Am I interrupting something?"

"No, no. John and I were just talking. John Smyth, this is Sergeant Troy Wesson of the local RCMP detachment."

"Yes, we've met," Smyth said. "We ran into each other at a rest stop when I was driving here from Prince George."

"A truck chain-up area, actually," Wesson said.

"Do you mind if John stays while we talk then?" the pastor asked.

"That depends. I don't want him publishing what I say to you."

"Oh no. This will be strictly off the record," Smyth said.

"You can trust John's discretion," the pastor affirmed.

"I will even take the batteries out of my tape recorder if you like," Smyth said. Seeing Wesson's puzzled look, he explained, "I was interviewing Paul earlier, and I taped it for editing later on."

"I have kind of a theological question," Wesson began.

"Oh, then John should definitely stay," Paul said. "He knows as much theology as I do."

"The question is, do you think witches are real?"

"That depends on what you mean by witches," the pastor said. "Witches don't necessarily look like the common conception—with black hats, warts, black cats, and brooms. But we believe there really are such things as evil spirits, and some people do align themselves with these evil spirits or demons, and some of them call themselves witches. There are also people who are possessed by evil spirits. The demons are inside them and control them."

"What do you think these evil spirits can do? Can they kill people?"

"Well, maybe by making them sick."

"Could an evil spirit make someone kill someone else?"

"Yes. That's possible. Some killers may certainly be possessed by demons."

"You know we're investigating these murders." Wesson paused, breathed in, and continued. "Someone has killed two people, a man and a woman, cut them up into pieces, mutilated the faces, and dumped their bodies in the bush beside the road. It was a terrible thing to do. Could a bad spirit have forced somebody to do something like that?"

"Yes, but not necessarily," Paul responded. "Christians believe that the world is fallen, which means God created it good, but people messed it up by choosing to do bad things. The evil stemming from that one act then ricochets and overlaps in all kinds of ways. Demons do encourage people to do bad things, but people also do bad things on their own. Demons sometimes control people, but the people have to open themselves up to that control first, to invite the demons into their lives."

"What we're saying," John Smyth broke in, "is that demons *can* do evil, but that most of the evil in this world is not done by demonic forces but by ordinary people who deliberately choose to do something they know is wrong. One of my seminary professors reminded us once that when we look at the crucifixion of Jesus—the most evil deed in the history of humanity—we see he was not murdered by demons or madmen. He was murdered by ordinary, respectable men who chose to do something wrong for very practical reasons. They murdered him because they saw him as a threat to their political power. They knew it was unjust, but they figured he was only one person and it didn't really matter. They had no idea that anyone would ever know the details of what they had done. They figured he would be dead and forgotten."

"The thing is," Wesson said, "you can't tell this to anyone. Last week I saw someone who seems to be a witch cutting the limbs off little dolls with an electric knife. Could that result in a real person being cut up?"

"Not by itself, it couldn't," Pastor Paul responded. "One of my seminary professors told me that we must avoid two extremes. One is assuming that demons have no power—because they do have power. But the other is assuming they have unlimited power and then living in fear. We need to remember that the Holy Spirit, the Spirit of Jesus, is much more powerful than all the demons in the world put together. If we have the Spirit of Jesus in us, then he will protect us against evil forces, and we don't have to be afraid."

That's what you get for asking church people questions, Wesson thought. *Ask a simple question and you get a sermon in response.* His mind kept playing over and over the image of Mary Pendragon kneeling before her candles and cutting the arms and legs off figurines. There had been seven such figurines, and the seventh appeared to be dressed in a red RCMP uniform.

"I would like to ask you something else," he said out loud. "Mr. Smyth told me that you spend one day a week out in the woods?"

"Well, not necessarily a whole day. I usually just spend Monday afternoons. What happened is that one day I went out for a hike up the side of the mountain. I'd had kind of a tough weekend, and I needed to get away. Anyway, I sat down and started to look out over the town and the valley, and I started to pray; and, well, it was such a meaningful time, I just decided to do it every Monday."

"You can't do it every Monday. This is Prince Rupert. What do you do when it rains?"

"Oh, I take rain gear and warm clothing. The hike alone is good for me. And that first Monday I found a rock overhang. It's not exactly a cave, but it is sheltered from the rain and wind. If the weather's really bad, I don't stay as long."

"You go to the same place every week?"

"Yes, usually."

"Do you ever go out to the chain-up area about thirty-five kilometers outside town?"

"Where you found the cut-up bodies? No."

"But if you were out in the woods alone, no one would know where you were, would they?"

Pastor Paul was finally at a loss for words.

"Pastor, you see a lot of people, right? Have you ever seen either of these people, either in the woods or anywhere else?" Wesson handed over copies of the facial reconstructions.

Pastor Paul took the pictures and looked at them dutifully. "I've seen these pictures in the paper, but no, I don't recognize either of them."

"Are you sure?"

"Yes. Has anybody else recognized them?"

Wesson paused. "No. We've been showing the pictures around town, but nobody seems to know them. I have another question for you. In your weekly visits to the woods, have you ever seen anything suspicious?"

"No, I don't think so."

"Do you see other people out in the woods?"

"Occasionally, but not often. No one else seems to come up to the rock overhang. That's one of the reasons I go there."

"Do you remember seeing anyone in particular?"

"No. Usually I just see people from a distance."

"Did you ever, for instance, see Dr. Haquapar?"

"Dr. Charles Haquapar? No. But I'm not sure I'd even know him on sight. We heard—well, we go to another doctor."

"Do you ever hear chainsaws in the woods? Or see anybody with a chainsaw?"

"No, I don't recall seeing anyone with a chainsaw, at least in the woods where I go. I might have heard a chainsaw, but I don't know. Around here, a chainsaw is just background noise. I don't know whether I would even notice it."

"Thank you," Wesson said. "You have been very helpful. You will let me know if you ever do see or hear anything suspicious?" He got up from the pew where he had been sitting and turned toward the door.

"Sergeant," Smyth asked, "is the witch you mentioned one of the suspects?"

"You can't write about that," Wesson said.

"I won't, but I'm just curious. Is this person a suspect?"

"No more than several other people," Wesson said. "Look. I asked for a theological opinion, but that doesn't mean I want you involved in the case. You take care of the church and leave crime investigation to the police."

"I helped solve a murder once," Smyth said. "Back in Winnipeg."

"Being a witness is not the same thing as being an investigator."

Smyth was silent a moment. "You don't think we would make a good crime-fighting team? We've got the right names for it."

"Names?"

"Smyth and Wesson."

Wesson, prepared to argue, had not been ready for this.

"Seriously," Pastor Paul said, "we won't get involved in the murder investigation, but we will pray for you. We will pray that you find out who the murderer is, and we will also pray that you will be protected from evil forces."

"Thank you," Wesson said. "But it will be hard work that solves this case, not prayer."

Chapter 12

MONDAY, MAY 31

On Monday, Wesson decided to spend the day in the office. A phrase kept running through his head: "We often look at things from the wrong perspective." Leblanc, Johnson, and Rumple had gone out around seven to set up their roadblock. Archbold was working the phone.

Around ten o'clock, Archbold knocked on his door. "Boss, I got the report on Gerard Hawkins from Williams Lake."

"What's it say?"

Archbold sat down in a chair facing Wesson, leaned back, and crossed his long legs. "You can read it yourself, but basically what it says is that about five years ago, our Mr. Hawkins was living down in Cariboo country, doing pretty much what he does now. He was married to a Japanese woman, a bit younger than him. No kids. One evening, the wife drives down to the store. It's wet, the car skids off the road, but she isn't going very fast, so she's not badly hurt, they think. But along comes a gang of kids high on crystal meth. They rape her and beat her to death. They're all young offenders, so the longest sentence is three years. After the trial, Hawkins sells his place and moves up here."

Wesson was silent for a few moments. "No wonder he's got an attitude."

"If they did that to my wife, I'd be more bitter than he is."

"Maybe. How do we know how bitter he is?"

At twelve thirty, Leblanc called in from the roadblock.

"How's it going?" Wesson asked.

"There's a lot of angry motorists out here, but none of them so far has recognized either of the victims."

"So, you've got nothing? Keep going till the end of the shift, and then we'll reevaluate for tomorrow."

"I didn't say we had nothing. About ten minutes ago, I talked to a trucker. He said a while back he saw a small red pickup parked in a rest stop."

"And?"

"And a man came out of the woods carrying a jigsaw. He was wearing goggles and had a plastic poncho under his arm."

"When did the trucker see this?"

"What I said—a while back. I asked him to be more precise, and he said a few weeks or months—he doesn't remember. A while back."

"What time of day?"

"He doesn't remember that, either. He thinks it might have been early morning or evening—he thinks the man was in shadows."

"So he didn't get a good look at him."

"Of course not. He was in shadows and wearing goggles."

"Was this at the chain-up area?"

"Might be or might be some other rest stop. He doesn't think it was here, but he's not sure."

"Where does he think it might have been?"

"He doesn't remember. He isn't even sure it was on this highway. He's pretty sure it was in British Columbia."

"I didn't expect it was at some rest stop surrounded by trees and mountains in Saskatchewan. But it could have been at the chain-up area?"

"Yeah, it could have been. He doesn't remember."

Wesson sighed. "Does he remember anything more about the truck?"

"No, just small and red. And kind of beat-up."

"I suppose from the cab of a big rig, any pickup would look small. Did the man get into the small red truck?"

"He doesn't know. He was just pulling out of the rest stop himself."

"Why didn't he report this earlier?"

"He didn't connect it to the chainsaw murders. This guy didn't have a chainsaw. He didn't think it was relevant."

"Yeah, well, he may be right about that. Did you get the trucker's name?"

"Yeah. Vernon Wright, an owner-operator working for Long Run Trucking Company, based in Calgary."

"Okay. Anything else?"

"Nope. That's it."

"Okay, keep at it."

Wesson sat for a moment thinking about beach balls and high-society dances. Then he phoned Dr. Decoran at the lab in Vancouver.

"Doc, I've got a question for you. Were the bodies necessarily cut up by a chainsaw?"

"No. If you read my original report, I said the bodies were cut up by a high-speed saw. There are saw marks on the bones. They could have been made by a chainsaw, but they could also have been made by another kind of saw—and there are marks made by animals as well. Once we are sure which are saw marks, we will start comparing them to the marks made by various kinds of saws, including various brands of chainsaws. When we have it figured out, we'll let you know."

"Would this kind of cutting require medical knowledge?"

"A basic knowledge of human anatomy would help, to know where the joints are—but it wouldn't be necessary, and it certainly wouldn't require a high degree of surgical skill."

"Thanks, Doc."

Wesson put down the phone, went to the door, and yelled, "Archie!"

A few moments later, Corporal Archbold was seated in Wesson's office with the door closed. Wesson told him about the phone calls, then said, "Archie, I want you to do a full background check on Dr. Haquapar. What was he doing before he came here? Does he have a record, or, more likely, have there been any investigations into his conduct?"

"Okay. He's got a small red truck. Do you really think he could have done it? Decoran said the killer didn't require a high degree of surgical skill."

"That would fit Haquapar. Look, I don't know if he could have done it or not. There's not much evidence pointing his way, and I'm not ready to question him now. If he is guilty, that would just warn him to cover up what evidence there is. We certainly don't have enough right now to justify a search warrant, but let's see what you find out first. In the meantime, I think I may go out and help with the roadblock, maybe reduce the number of angry motorists."

Having said that, Wesson continued to sit in his chair. "You know what else strikes me?" he asked.

"What?"

"This whole investigation is a fluke."

"You're not happy with the way we're approaching it?"

"No. I think we're doing our jobs well enough. It's just a matter of following proper procedure. No, I was thinking of the beginning. The little girl went a few feet into the bush and peed on a finger. But the finger wasn't supposed to be there. We didn't find any other body parts in that particular spot, on the level ground near the chain-up area, except one other finger. All of the other parts had been taken to the edge of the slope and thrown down. I think maybe that finger was dropped near the chain-up area by mistake. If it hadn't been dropped there and if the girl hadn't gone into the woods at that exact spot or hadn't noticed the finger, chances are the bodies would never have been found. They would have decomposed, been covered up with leaves, been eaten or dragged away by animals. If it wasn't for that fluky finger, we wouldn't be conducting a murder investigation at all."

Wesson drove out along the highway. About twenty-five kilometers from town, he pulled into a small parking lot beside the highway with room for about a dozen cars. From this point, four hiking trails fanned out into the forest, and the lot was there for hikers' cars. Two cars were parked there today—a green Honda and an ancient Chevy of indeterminate color. Wesson sat and thought for a few minutes, then pulled back onto the highway and drove on.

Half a kilometer from the chain-up area, he came to a full stop behind a long line of cars that was slowly inching its way forward. He checked his watch, drummed his fingers on the steering wheel, and inched forward along with the other cars.

When Wesson reached the chain-up area at last, Leblanc leaned into the window and grinned. "Checking up on us—or come to help?"

Wesson let out a deep breath. "The line goes back about half a kilometer, takes about fifteen minutes."

Leblanc nodded.

"Have you got any more leads?"

"Not me. I haven't checked with Johnson or Rumple in the past few minutes, but the last I checked, they didn't either. So, are you going to stay and help shorten the line?"

"No, I don't think so," Wesson said. "Maybe later. There's something else I want to check."

Wesson drove on another ten kilometers until he reached a rest stop, a wide paved area on the south side of the highway with several litter barrels and two small pit toilets just off the edge of the pavement. Three cars and two RVs were parked here, and a dozen people milled around stretching their legs, changing drivers, eating snack foods, and visiting the toilets.

Wesson pulled into a parking space near one end of the paved area. He sat and thought for a few minutes, then got out and locked his car. He walked around the car as unobtrusively as possible, stepped over the guardrail, and walked down into the forest. The underbrush was dense in spots, and he had to pick his way, looking for the more open areas where the walking was easier. He weaved back and forth, following the open places, doubling back, making as little noise as possible, being careful to avoid stepping over a drop-off into the valley below, and gradually working his way around the rest stop to cover an area up to about thirty feet from the pavement.

Policemen cannot do anything unobtrusively. By the time Wesson emerged from the woods at the far end of the rest area, somewhat dirty and disheveled, there were eight vehicles in the parking lot and twenty people milling around watching his car and the spot where he had gone down into the bush. Without saying a word, he walked across the wide paved area, got into his car, and pulled back onto the highway.

About ten kilometers farther on was another rest stop, this one on the north side of the highway. No vehicles were parked here. Pulling into a space in the middle of the paved area, Wesson walked down into the woods and repeated the procedure of weaving through the bush. After about twenty minutes, at a spot about twenty feet from one end of the pavement, where the ground sloped down into a side valley, he stopped, knelt down, and examined something in the brush. Straightening, he made his way back to his car and picked up the handset for his radio.

Chapter 13

TUESDAY, JUNE 1

The search and forensics teams began at seven on Tuesday morning and worked until after eight that evening. The ground being searched included the small amount of relatively flat ground around the rest stop, a couple of hundred feet of the adjacent mountainside, and both slopes of the side valley at one end of the rest stop—but it was only in the side valley that they found anything.

An hour or two after the search had started, the group of reporters began to assemble at the end of the rest stop opposite the end where the side valley was. Before the day was done, there were nine of them, counting three cameramen. At five o'clock, Wesson went over and talked to them.

"We are not going to be issuing any news releases or making any statements today," he said.

"Did you find another body?" Melanie Grayson, the Vancouver TV reporter, asked.

"Yes, I can confirm that we have found human remains."

"How many bodies?" asked Jason Thuringer, the stringer for the Vancouver newspaper.

"We are not releasing that information at this time." There appeared to be four, but Wesson was not taking any chances on being wrong this time. "We haven't finished our search of the area yet."

"But there is more than one?"

"Yes."

"What's the problem?" Thuringer asked. "Are they so badly cut up you don't know how many there are?"

"It's just that we haven't finished searching."

"Well, how many have you found so far?"

"That's all we are saying for today. We'll give you more information tomorrow."

Wesson turned and walked away. The reporters had been counting the body bags brought up, but as they did not know how many pieces the bodies had been cut into, they could not know how many bodies there were.

John Smyth had gone through the police roadblock at the chain-up area on Monday morning on his way back to Prince George, telling a pretty young constable named Johnson that he had seen nothing and that Sergeant Wesson had already questioned him. His plane had landed back in Winnipeg very late on Monday evening.

On Tuesday, for once, he decided to take a day off in compensation for his weekend's work.

"Ruby," he said that afternoon, "why don't we pick the kids up after school and go to Assiniboine Park for a picnic?"

The three youngest children were bouncing with excitement, but twelve-year-old Michael declared himself bored by such family activities. John himself had had trouble relaxing as his mind strayed repeatedly to the grisly remains discovered along a desolate highway in British Columbia. Sitting in the sun on a blanket next to Ruby while the younger children ran and squealed and Michael wandered aimlessly nearby, Smyth found himself thinking of the grief facing the families of the victims. Would the evil unleashed in that area hinder the renewal in the Prince Rupert church? Or would the fear actually help with renewal, as people were driven to seek answers for big questions?

Ruby nudged him. "You look lost in thought."

"I was just wondering," he said, "if anything good could ever come out of a murder."

Chapter 14

WEDNESDAY, JUNE 2

When the phone rang early Wednesday afternoon, John Smyth was at his desk, attempting to make a dent in the work that had piled up while he was away. Still distracted by thoughts of his weekend in Prince Rupert, he let the phone ring several times before he realized it was for him and picked up the receiver.

"John, it's Elvira," said a breathless voice on the other end of the line.

"Elvira, are you all right?"

"John, I have a big favor to ask you. Mr. Parkinson just called me. He wants me to go down to see him at his office. I have a feeling it might be bad news. Maybe he is going to tell me he is going to stop paying Jake's salary. Maybe . . . I don't know. But I don't think I can face it alone. John, would you go with me?"

Smyth took a look at the mound of paper smothering his desk. He reflected that a woman who apparently had trouble facing so many things apparently had no trouble getting him to do things for her. Maybe that was the secret of her strength—she knew how and when to get the help she needed. He sighed. "Of course, Elvira," he said. "I will come and pick you up."

He made a phone call to Ruby, and they decided after a hurried discussion that Ruby would not go along. The children would be home from school soon, there was not time to find a babysitter, and while Michael was old enough to care for the three younger children, they did not feel comfortable leaving him in charge. Besides, they didn't know how long the meeting might take or how complicated it might become. Accordingly, John walked quickly the few blocks home, dropped a briefcase bulging with work in the front hall, kissed Ruby, and took the car.

Elvira was waiting by the door when he arrived. Other than a quick "Thank you for coming," they rode in silence.

The contrast between the stately homes in Elvira's neighborhood and the industrial area by the railway tracks was quite startling. John had never been to Winnipack before, but he aimed the car in the direction of the big stone towers, and Elvira gave brief directions for the last few turns until they arrived in a visitors' parking lot.

The stone towers looked much as they always had, except for the addition of the bright orange logo. The lower buildings beside them, however, had been completely renovated. The two-story office wing faced the road and the visitors' parking lot, with a new brick façade and large tinted windows. A sickly sweet smell of manure and offal wafted toward them from the holding pens and slaughterhouses at the back, though the odor was surprisingly mild for a packinghouse. Grant Parkinson reportedly insisted on strict "environmental controls"—another reason for his popularity in the city.

Elvira led the way tentatively through double doors into the main lobby. It was spacious and bright, with modern artwork and a staircase in one corner curving up to the second floor.

A crisp receptionist said, "Good afternoon, Mrs. Rempel. I'll tell Mr. Parkinson you are here."

A few moments later, a middle-aged woman in a dark business suit, a white blouse, medium-height black shoes, and short blonde hair descended the stairs. "Good afternoon, Elvira. I'll take you up to Mr. Parkinson."

"Um . . . this is my friend, John Smyth. I would like him to come too."

The woman looked John Smyth over. He was suddenly aware that his shoes needed polishing and that he had bought his sports jacket at a garage sale. "Certainly," the woman said. She turned and led the way up the stairs.

The lobby was in one corner of the building. The stairs led to a long hall that ran along the front of the building. To the left as he walked, Smyth saw secretaries whose open work spaces sported large tinted windows facing the parking lot. On his right were a row of executive offices with closed cherry-wood doors. As he passed one office where the door was open, he saw that the executive offices were large, richly furnished, and fitted with large windows looking out over the meat-cutting and processing plant.

"That's Jake's office," Elvira whispered. Something seemed to catch in her throat, and she whispered even more quietly, "Was."

The woman stopped at the very last office and ushered Elvira and Smyth through the door. It was as beautifully furnished as Jake's office, with cherry furniture and a royal blue plush carpet, but it was twice the size. A tall man with dark brown hair came forward to greet them. His suit was expensive and tailored, and he looked even more handsome in person than he did on television.

"Welcome, Elvira. How are you doing?" His voice was refined, his manner charming. He had taken Elvira's hand and was looking kindly into her eyes.

"I'm fine, Mr. Parkinson. This is my friend John Smyth."

Parkinson raised quizzical eyebrows and looked at Smyth.

"We're in the same care group," Smyth explained. "From church. It's a group of people who get together regularly for prayer and Bible study. My wife and I lead it."

"Oh," Parkinson said with a small smile. "Well, I'm glad someone is watching out for Elvira." Then, indicating the fourth person in the room—the woman in the dark business suit having quietly left the room, closing the door behind her—he said, "Elvira, I think you may have met Mark Driemer? Mark is one of the drivers for Winnipack."

John remembered Driemer from the picture in Jake's pocket. Tall and good-looking, wearing well-tailored casual clothes, he shook hands with John Smyth and Elvira.

"Won't you sit down?" Parkinson indicated a group of comfortable chairs in the corner of the room. "Can I get you any coffee? Water?"

"No, thank you," Elvira responded.

"Elvira, have you heard anything from Jake yet?" Parkinson asked.

"No," Elvira responded. "I'm afraid I haven't. The children and I are very worried."

"I know you must be," Parkinson said. He paused. "I asked you to come today because Mark came to me with some information that we agreed we should pass on to you."

Driemer cleared his throat. "Mrs. Rempel, I have something to tell you, and I hope you'll understand why I didn't tell you before." He took a deep breath and continued. "I owe a

144

lot to Jake. He took a chance on me when no one else would. He took me on as an apprentice driver and helped me get the training I needed, even paid for it and said I could pay him back once I started driving full-time."

"Yes. That's the kind of thing Jake would do," Elvira said.

"A couple of months ago," Driemer continued, "I was getting ready for a trip out to the port in Prince Rupert, leaving in the evening. Jake knew the schedule, of course. Jake came to me that afternoon as I was picking up the paperwork and asked me to take him along. He said he had to go to Prince George on personal business, and he didn't want anyone to know about it. He said he might be gone a few weeks, but that he would come back. He stressed it was important that I not tell anyone. It sounded kind of odd, not really like Jake, but I owed him a lot, and I agreed to do what he asked. I took Jake out as far as Prince George, dropped him off at the edge of town, and continued on to Prince Rupert. When I got back, I left right away on another trip—I think one of the other drivers was sick or something—and it was after I got back from that one that I found out you'd reported him missing. Anyway, I had made a promise to Jake not to tell anyone, and I kept expecting him to come back or contact you. But two months have gone by, and I was starting to get worried, so I finally decided to tell Mr. Parkinson and ask his advice."

"And I said he should tell you immediately," Grant Parkinson finished. "So here we are. Elvira, I am sorry Mark didn't tell you this earlier. I hope it will help you find Jake, give the police some idea where to look."

Elvira turned back to Driemer. "I can understand you wanted to keep your promise to Jake, but when you found out about the hundred thou—"

"Elvira," Parkinson broke in, "I haven't told Mark or anyone else about that."

"Oh, of course. Mr. Driemer, did Jake say anything to you about his cousin?"

"His cousin? No."

"Did Jake take anything with him?" Smyth asked.

"He had a small bag, sort of a duffel bag. I don't know what was in it. I assume it just had some clothes and a toothbrush, like what truckers take with them."

"Where did you drop him off in Prince George?" Smyth continued.

"At a gas station on the edge of town. After I dropped him off, he went over to a pay phone, and that's the last I saw of him. I didn't stay long enough to see if he actually phoned someone. But I do remember wondering why he didn't have his cell phone with him."

"Jake never liked cell phones," Elvira said quietly. "We had one for the car, but he always forgot to take it with him."

"Did he say anything on the trip out?" Smyth asked Driemer.

"Not really. He seemed tired, and he slept some of the way. We talked about the weather and the traffic and truck driving—nothing that seems important. Once when we stopped, he made a phone call. I assumed he was phoning Mrs. Rempel or someone like that."

"Did he say anything about his car?" Elvira asked suddenly.

"His car? No. He came walking in through the yard gates just as I was about to leave. I hadn't been watching, so I assumed maybe you had dropped him off, or maybe he had parked the car on a side street."

"It was found a couple of days later in a parking lot near the bus terminal," Smyth said.

"I don't know anything about that," Driemer answered.

"If he had parked it on a side street in this part of town, the car could have been stolen by someone who wanted to get to the bus terminal or even by kids going for a joyride," Parkinson said.

"Or maybe he parked near the bus terminal and took a city bus here," Driemer suggested.

"There weren't any fingerprints on the car," Elvira said. "Except Jake's, I mean."

Driemer shrugged. "I really don't know about that."

There was a long silence as they all absorbed what they had heard.

"I'm really sorry, Mrs. Rempel," Driemer finally said. "I thought I was doing what was best for Jake. I am willing to tell all this to the police if you want."

"Elvira," Parkinson asked, "are the police still investigating Jake's disappearance? We weren't sure who to call. I can't remember the name of the detective I talked to before. Do you have it?"

"I am not sure that the police ever investigated Jake's disappearance very seriously, and I doubt they are doing anything now at all. But I think I still have the detective's card at home somewhere. Thank you, Mr. Driemer, for telling me all this. I understand why you didn't tell me before. John, I think I would like to go home now."

Smyth helped her to her feet. She seemed quite shaken.

"I am very sorry about all this," Parkinson said as he opened the door for them. "If there is anything I can do, please let me know."

"Thank you," she mumbled. Smyth held her arm as they walked down the hall and stairs. She stumbled slightly on the way out to the car.

"Elvira, are you all right?" John asked when they were in the car. "Should I drive you to a doctor or the hospital? You don't look well."

Elvira breathed deeply. "I am all right, John, physically. It

147

is just that it was such a shock. If we had only known this two months ago, maybe we could have found Jake before it was too late."

"Don't give up, Elvira. It still may not be too late. By the way, why did you ask about Jake's cousin?"

"Jake's cousin Abe went hunting with a friend up near Prince George last fall. They went into the bush and never came out again. There was a search, but they never found them. Of course, by then they had been missing for over two weeks. They might not have been reported missing even then if Abe hadn't failed to show up for Jake's sixtieth birthday party."

Smyth absorbed this information. "Was Abe ever found?"
"No."

"Do you think Jake might have gone out looking for him? Maybe Abe is still alive and phoned him to come out."

"I thought of that, but if that was the case, why didn't Jake tell me? We talked about everything."

"Maybe Abe asked him not to."

"But surely Jake wouldn't just go out into the forest look-ing for Abe. He could have gotten lost, and we wouldn't even know where to look." Elvira began to sob gently. Smyth put his arm around her shoulders.

When the crying had subsided, Smyth said, "Elvira, I real-ly think you should tell all this to the police. Shall we go back to your place and get the detective's card?"

"I remember his name. He was a Detective Harder, a young man with the Winnipeg Police Department."

Smyth knew that in Elvira's terms, "young" could mean anyone under forty.

"He was a very disagreeable man, John. I don't want to talk to him again."

"Why? What did he do?"

"He just seemed arrogant and unfeeling. He was cruel. He kept asking me how our marriage was, whether Jake was having an affair with a younger woman, who Jake's favorite secretary was, how often he went to casinos and bars, whether he ever went anywhere without telling me, if we were having financial problems, whether he took anyone with him on business trips. It was awful—just made things worse."

"But all policemen have to ask questions like that, be suspicious of everyone. People lie to them all the time."

"But he wasn't suspicious of everyone, just of me and Jake. He even suggested I wasn't a very good wife to Jake, that he wasn't . . . satisfied with me." She broke into sobs again.

Smyth was beginning to understand why Elvira had not talked very much about Jake's disappearance to the home Bible study group. When the sobbing subsided again, Smyth said, "Elvira, I have an idea. I need to find a phone booth."

"Sergeant Prestwyck," he yelled into the phone over the roar of traffic, wishing for the moment that he, too, had a company cell phone. "This is John Smyth." After a pause, he added, "The religious writer."

"Ah, Mr. Smyth," the sergeant responded, "seen any good crimes lately?" They had gotten to know one another the previous year, when Smyth witnessed a murder from the window of a descending plane.

"No," Smyth said now, "but I have a friend who needs some help. Can I come and see you?"

"Sure, but I will only be here for another hour."

"Fine. I'll be right there."

Smyth got back into his battered station wagon and headed for the Royal Canadian Mounted Police division headquarters on Portage Avenue. While crimes in Winnipeg fell under the jurisdiction of the Winnipeg Police Department, the RCMP policed the rest of the province of Manitoba as well as most other provinces in Canada.

Sergeant Robert Prestwyck was a tall, middle-aged, close-cropped, slightly paunchy career police officer with the RCMP. He looked just a bit untidy in spite of his clean tan-and-blue police uniform.

"Thank you for agreeing to see us, Sergeant Prestwyck," Smyth said. "This is my friend Elvira Rempel. Mrs. Rempel's husband, Jake, was the owner of Rempel Trucking Company, and then, when it merged with Winnipack, he became vice president in charge of transportation at Winnipack." From the expression on Prestwyck's face, Smyth surmised that he had never heard of Rempel Trucking Company but knew all about Winnipack. With Prestwyck, however, you could never be sure. "About two and a half months ago, Jake disappeared."

"Two and a half months ago? Why did you wait that long to notify the police?"

"Elvira did notify the police two and a half months ago. The Winnipeg police."

"If Mr. Rempel disappeared in Winnipeg, then it is the responsibility of the Winnipeg police to investigate it," Prestwyck said. "Why come to me?"

"Just today, one of the drivers for the company told us that on the night Jake disappeared, he drove Jake to Prince George, B.C., and dropped him off there. That would be RCMP jurisdiction, wouldn't it?"

"Yes, but if the disappearance was originally reported to the Winnipeg police, that is where you should have taken this new information. Then they would have contacted us if they needed help. It's best to have all the information collected in one place."

"Sergeant," Elvira said, "my husband was a good man. We

had a good marriage, we talked about everything, we trusted each other. That detective from the Winnipeg Police Department didn't believe any of that. He just assumed that Jake was a high-living businessman who ran off with a mistress. He didn't even try to find Jake. But Jake wouldn't just run off like that. I think something awful has happened to him."

"Please, Sergeant Prestwyck," Smyth added.

"All right," Prestwyck said. "Give me some more details, especially about this truck driver. I'll contact the Winnipeg police and ask to see the file. Then I'll see what I can do."

On Wednesday morning, on Sergeant Wesson's orders, search teams had begun general surveys of the bush around every rest stop and chain-up area between Prince Rupert and Prince George. Inspector Travis had readily endorsed the plan as soon as the first body parts were found at the second site on Tuesday. Meanwhile, Johnson, Leblanc, and Rumple spent Wednesday morning working the roadblock at the chain-up area where the first bodies had been found. By early afternoon, however, they packed it up in order to gather for a task force meeting. The six of them—Wesson, Archbold, Leblanc, Johnson, Rumple, and Simmons—squeezed into a small meeting room at the station.

"Pierre," Wesson began, "how did the roadblock go today? Did you get any leads?"

Leblanc replied, "There were a few comments we thought worth writing down for our reports, but I don't think we got anything likely at all." The other two nodded in agreement.

"Well, try a couple more days. There are different truckers coming and going every day, and we're really looking for a needle in a haystack, hoping to get lucky. Archie, what have you found out?"

Archbold shrugged. "You asked me to check on a lot of

different things. First, unlike the chain-up area, there is no record of anybody living within three kilometers either way of the rest stop where we found the new bodies."

"That doesn't mean no one is there," Johnson objected. "The old man Isaac wasn't on any records as living near the chain-up area either, but Sergeant Wesson found him there anyway."

"True," Archbold responded. "I guess somebody will have to do a visual search, eh, Boss?"

"Probably," Wesson said.

At a nod from Wesson, Archbold continued, "Second, I didn't find out anything more from the police down in Cariboo country, but I phoned the Williams Lake newspaper and asked them to check their files. Ten years ago, it seems, Gerard Hawkins beat the snot out of some guy who had insulted his wife. It was reported in the paper in a profile they did on Hawkins's sculptures, but the victim never reported it to the police, so it never showed up in their files."

"Did they give you the name of the guy he beat up?" Wesson asked.

"It's not in the story, and the reporter who wrote the story was killed in a car crash two years ago."

"Anything suspicious about the car crash?" Wesson asked.

"Not that I know of, but I'm still checking."

"What do you think—the victim showed up around here seeking revenge, and Hawkins killed him?" Rumple asked.

"It's a possibility," Wesson said, "but no more than that."

"Are the people who live near the chain-up area still suspects anyway?" Johnson asked. "The only reason we focused on them is that they lived near the place where the first bodies were found, but now we've found bodies in another area."

"One of them could still have killed the first two bodies, dumped them close to home, then killed some others and dumped them farther away just to throw us off," Archbold suggested.

"We only looked at them originally as witnesses," Wesson said. "They could still be that, but I wouldn't rule them out as suspects, either, any more than anyone else."

"Third," Archbold continued, "I started looking into the background of Dr. Haquapar. It's not easy because the medical societies keep their records sealed, but I am working on some other angles and might have something by tomorrow or Friday."

No one commented on this.

"And fourth, the lab in Vancouver is still checking the DNA of the first two victims against the DNA of various missing persons, but there are no positive results yet. It's a lengthy process, and there is a backlog of other cases. Gracie Levasseur is still officially missing, and I haven't gotten anywhere looking for Luther Malone. I haven't been able to trace Amber Long either. Her family still lives in Calgary, but they are evidently out of town, and no one seems to know where."

"Anything else?" Wesson asked.

Archbold shook his head.

"Any ideas anybody wants to share?"

The others sat in silence.

"Okay," Wesson continued. "I have just received the very preliminary results from the new bodies we sent to Vancouver. There are four of them—three men and a woman. They seem to all have been killed about the same time. All four were cut up as before, fingertips and faces mangled. And they were frozen like the others, but probably not for as long, then thawed out about two weeks before they were found.

"All were killed in the same way, with a sharp instrument driven into the skull, although the three men also sustained some other injuries, in one case a possibly unrelated skull fracture. The woman was probably in her forties, with dyed blonde hair—about one-point-seven-two meters or five foot eight, weight about fifty-nine kilograms, a hundred thirty pounds. The second is a man in his late fifties or early sixties, about one-point-eight-three meters or six feet tall, weight about ninety kilograms or two hundred pounds. The third is a man in his fifties, one-point-seven-two meters, five foot eight, weight fifty-two kilograms, a hundred fifteen pounds. The fourth is another man, also in his fifties, one-point-seven-five meters, five foot nine, weight fifty kilograms, a hundred ten—"

"Wow, those last two—" Leblanc broke in.

"Wait till I'm finished," Wesson ordered. "The last two show signs of malnutrition and other health problems. The woman and the last two had traces of alcohol in their systems. There will be more details later." Turning to Leblanc, he said, "Pierre, you wanted to say something?"

"Just that the last two sounded rather thin."

"Yeah. Any other thoughts?"

"Could the last two be the missing hunters?" Archbold asked. "Maybe they hid out or were lost in the woods all winter, starving, and then were killed in the spring. That would explain why they were so thin."

Wesson considered. "It's a possibility, but who are the other two?" When no one spoke, he added, "I'll have the lab check it out. Any other ideas?"

They all sat for a while pondering the possibilities, but no one said anything further.

"Okay," Wesson said. "I have called a press conference for six o'clock, where I will read the statement I just gave you. I hope to have facial reconstructions by tomorrow, when I will call another press conference. And then we can really get to work."

Wesson read the same information to the ten assembled reporters, describing the victims but omitting the information about how they were killed. Assembled in front of the police station this time because they would not all fit inside, the reporters seemed almost as much at a loss for words as the police officers.

Almost, but not quite.

"Does this mean that there is a serial killer operating in this area?" Melanie Grayson asked.

"It looks like it," Wesson conceded.

"Could there be other bodies at other places along the highway?"

"It is possible, but we have no reason to believe that is the case."

"Are you searching other places along the highway?"

"Yes, and so far we have found no other bodies."

"Why did you search the area where you found the second group of bodies?" This was Jason Thuringer's question.

Wesson hesitated. No other police officer had asked him that question yet. They had all been too busy. How could he answer? There was the information that a trucker had seen someone, perhaps Dr. Haquapar, coming out of the woods at a spot that might have been different. But that tip had been vague at best. The truth was, Wesson didn't know why he had begun searching other spots along the highway. It had been just a hunch, a wild guess, a compelling hint from some back corner of his brain. He didn't really know where the idea had come from, but how could he tell the reporters that? Instead, he said, "We are not releasing that information at this time."

"Are the police using a profiler to determine the characteristics of the chainsaw killer?" Melanie Grayson again.

"Not yet. We will probably do that after we have more

information about the most recent victims." The truth was that Wesson had not thought of it.

"Are other people in this area in danger? Is the chainsaw killer likely to kill again?"

That was the question. Wesson's answer was considered. "We are advising people to use caution, to be alert to unusual activity and to be wary of strangers, but there is no reason to panic. There have been six victims, but we would like to remind the public that that is over the course of several months. Police have increased their presence along the highway."

The last was true, not because patrols had increased but because Wesson and his investigators had been making so many trips up the highway.

Chapter 15

THURSDAY, JUNE 3

The dog teams and searchers had so far not found any more bodies along the highway. The lab had not yet provided any more information. Leblanc, Johnson, and Rumple were out running the roadblock again. And Wesson was restless.

At nine o'clock, Inspector Travis phoned. "I'm still tied up with this reorganization," he complained. "I could be here another month. How is the investigation into the chainsaw murders going?"

Wesson took stock. "It is just a matter of routine hard work. We are checking leads, looking for new leads, asking questions, checking backgrounds, analyzing evidence."

"Do you think you are close to solving the murders?"

"You never know when you get a break, but I would say that we are still probably weeks away at this point. We are making progress, but it is slow. And finding the new bodies is a complication."

"Get it done as fast as possible. The public is getting anxious, which means bad publicity for the police, the province, and Prince Rupert. People down here are worried about a detrimental effect on tourism, and the provincial government is starting to put some pressure on."

"It would be good publicity for us if we solve it, sir."

"How about these new bodies? Remind me—how exactly were they found?"

"I found them, actually. That was just part of the routine, checking all possibilities."

"Have you found any more?"

"No. The search of all the rest stops along the highway should wrap up in a day or two. I am starting to get hopeful that they won't find any more. Of course, we're only checking the rest stops. There's seven hundred kilometers of highway, most of it with forest on both sides. Bodies could be dumped just about anywhere. We don't have the manpower to check it all."

"Right. Let's hope it doesn't come to that. Do you need any help on this?"

"The dogs and the forensics teams have been a great help. The only thing is: Do we have access to a profiler? It would be really helpful if we knew what kind of a killer we are looking for."

"We may be able to find one who is available. But it's pretty obvious who you're looking for, isn't it? This will be a psycho, a misfit, some loner who's been abused or traumatized or feels inadequate. He'll be finding his victims in the same way. They'll all turn out to be hitchhikers or hunters or people he found in a bar—something like that."

"You're thinking the killer's definitely a man, then?"

"Could be a woman, but in almost all of such cases, it turns out to be a man."

Wesson considered. "You're probably right." He had not handled many murder investigations, and it was good to get advice from someone more experienced.

"Keep me informed," Travis barked and was gone.

About eleven thirty that morning, Archbold appeared in the doorway of the private office. "Boss, I finally got somewhere with checking Dr. Haquapar's background. Do you know where he practiced before he came here?"

"Not a clue. I think he was already here when I arrived."

"Actually, he's only been here about eight years. Before that he worked in two or three places for a year or so each, and before that, right out of medical school, he worked in an abortion clinic in California."

"And I gather he didn't graduate at the top of his class?"

"Somebody has to graduate near the bottom."

"Any previous problems? Why did he move around so often?"

"I don't know yet. He was restless, maybe. At least one of them was only a one-year position in the first place, replacing somebody on leave. One person I talked to wouldn't go on record but strongly hinted that his drinking might have been a factor. The big piece of dirt is that when he was in California, there was an accusation that one of the aborted fetuses was born alive and Haquapar cut it up in order to kill it, pretending it had been pulled apart in the abortion process. All the doctors and nurses swore the fetus was already dead, so nothing came of it, but eight months later Haquapar left town."

"Can you match Haquapar's presence in the various places with any unsolved homicides?"

"Good question. I had asked the local police for any information on Haquapar, not about homicides in their areas. I'll go back and do that. Are you thinking he's a likely suspect?"

"I don't know. Check out the unsolved homicides. Meanwhile, I think we've got enough already to talk to him and probably even get a search warrant. Make the inquiries, then try for a search warrant for his office, house, and vehicle. We'll execute it tomorrow morning. There's something else I need to check out this afternoon."

After several days of unusually warm, sunny weather, Prince Rupert's weather had returned to its usual state—steady rain. The area was, after all, essentially a coastal rain forest, with the prevailing westerly winds continually bringing in moisture from the Pacific. Wesson had postponed his trip for most of the morning in the hope that the weather would clear, but it hadn't, and he knew that if he waited for good weather, he might be waiting for days.

Once again he drove out to the chain-up area thirty-five kilometers out of town. This time he parked on the other side of the road, up against the trees, so that his car could not be seen from any of the clearings above. He got out of the car, put on his rain poncho, and began clambering up through the woods. The ground was slippery and the climbing difficult, and he made even slower progress than the first time. In spite of the cold rain, he was soon sweating profusely under the poncho, his uniform getting wetter both inside and out. Eventually he struck the path, almost missing it in the rain. He paused for breath and then proceeded to Isaac's hut. He did not need to take as much care in approaching this time; the drumming rain drowned out all other sounds.

Smoke drifted from Isaac's chimney, although the rain drove it back down again to hover drearily all around the hut. The canvas flap was pulled down tightly against the rain. Wesson approached directly, looked the situation over, pounded his hand on the wooden slats, called "Isaac!" and then lifted the flap.

Isaac sat cross-legged at the back of the hut next to the stove, looking more ragged and thin than ever. He looked up startled, like an animal caught by headlights. The black-covered book he had been reading before was open on his lap.

"May I come in?" Wesson asked, squatting at the other end of the hut.

Isaac said nothing, just glared at him.

"How are you doing today, Isaac? Are you getting enough to eat?"

"I'm fine," Isaac answered after a long pause.

"The other day," Wesson continued, "you said that Hawk's woman had given you a bookmark."

"No, I didn't! Hawk's wife is dead."

"Oh, but you did. What did you mean? Who is the woman you saw? When did she give you the bookmark?"

"My wife is upstairs," Isaac said, his eyes wild.

"May I see the bookmark?"

"I don't have it. I lost it."

Wesson suddenly lurched forward and grabbed the book out of Isaac's hands. Isaac cried out in fear. Wesson calmly pulled out the bookmark before handing the book back to Isaac. The bookmark was a piece of white cardboard with flowers hand drawn on it and a big sun shining down on them. There were no other distinguishing marks.

"Where did the woman get the bookmark?" he asked Isaac. "Did she make it?"

Isaac was shivering and shaking his head. He began to mutter to himself.

"It's okay, Isaac. I won't hurt you. I will leave you now. Do you mind if I keep this?"

Isaac shook his head.

"I thought not. Good-bye, Isaac."

Wesson crawled out of the hut and carefully pushed the tarpaulin door back into place. The rain seemed to have eased somewhat, although the trees and bushes still dripped steadily. He shifted the poncho and began walking back down the path toward Hawkins's place. As he got closer, he tried to move cautiously, hoping to catch Hawkins at home. He could not hear Hawkins's chainsaw.

Reaching the edge of the clearing, he peered cautiously out from behind the underbrush. It was only then that he realized it had stopped raining completely. Hawkins stood in the clearing, surveying the valley with a pair of binoculars. Wesson suddenly felt foolish. He stepped out of the bush and walked toward Hawkins.

"Good afternoon, Mr. Hawkins."

Hawkins nodded but said nothing. He did not seem surprised by the policeman's sudden appearance. Maybe he was used to it by now.

"You keep track of what goes on in your neighborhood, don't you?"

"The world's full of dangers and opportunities, and we'll be sorry if we miss either one."

It was one of the longest sentences Wesson had heard Hawkins speak. He decided to ask something he had not planned to ask. "What do you know about Mary Pendragon?"

Hawkins pondered a moment. "Isaac says she's an evil woman who presides over midnight dances ending with unspeakable rites. Isaac is not a stupid man."

"Mary Pendragon knows things sometimes too. Do you think she really is in touch with evil spirits?"

Hawkins did not reply. He raised the binoculars and began scanning the ridge of the mountain to the west. Then he lowered the binoculars, handed them to Wesson, and pointed to a spot high on the ridge.

Wesson pointed the binoculars in the suggested direction and soon found what he was looking for, a large white object half hidden by the trees. "A satellite dish?"

"She's also got a police band radio."

"How do you know?"

Hawkins shrugged.

"Isaac also says that your woman gave him this bookmark."

The question was designed to catch Hawkins by surprise. He did not respond.

"I know what happened to your wife five years ago. Isaac never saw her. Who gave him the bookmark?"

Hawkins's posture became even more rigid. "A young woman. I picked her up on the road coming back from town last winter. She stayed three weeks."

"Then what happened to her?"

"She left."

"She left?"

"I drove her to Prince George."

"Did you have sex with her?"

"No."

"Is that why you killed her?"

Hawkins glared at him.

"What was her name?"

"She said her name was Gracie."

"Gracie Levasseur?"

Hawkins shrugged. "Just Gracie."

"Blonde, about five seven?"

Hawkins nodded.

"You lied to me. You said you lived alone here."

"She wasn't that important. And she's been gone a long time."

"Can you prove she left here safely?"

"Can you prove she was ever here?" Hawkins said mockingly.

Wesson turned and began walking down the long lane and back along the highway to his car. It had stopped raining, the sun had come out, and he took off his dripping poncho.

The facial reconstructions did not arrive till after six. Wesson scheduled a press conference for eight o'clock and handed out the pictures. He answered all questions with "We don't know yet" and "We are not releasing that information."

Chapter 16

FRIDAY, JUNE 4

The voice behind the door was fuzzy with sleep and perhaps a hangover. "Who is it?"

"Sergeant Wesson."

After a long minute the door swung open to reveal a man in sweatpants and a wrinkled T-shirt. His thinning hair stood out from his head in tufts. "What's the problem?" he was saying. "You have another finger you want identi—" He stopped, overwhelmed by the sight of three policemen.

"Dr. Haquapar," Wesson said, "I have a search warrant for your apartment, your office, and your truck." He offered a paper to Haquapar, who did not take it.

"This is ridiculous!" he sputtered. "What's this all about?"

"Let's sit down and talk about it," Wesson said.

"Talk about it! Talk about what?"

Corporal Archbold and Constable Simmons moved in beside the doctor and guided him to a seat at the kitchen table.

Wesson sat down opposite him while the other two began a search of the apartment.

"Dr. Haquapar," Wesson said, "you have been seen on several occasions going into the woods out along the highway."

"So? It's illegal to take a walk in the woods?"

"Dr. Haquapar, you were positively identified coming out of the woods wearing a blood-soaked poncho and carrying a jigsaw."

Wesson saw fear on Haquapar's face. "This is ridiculous," he repeated.

"You were still positively identified."

Haquapar was quiet for a while, his brow knit in concentration. He reached for the search warrant and read it carefully. "You're going to search my apartment, office, and truck?"

Wesson nodded.

Haquapar said evenly, "It's not a jigsaw. It's a battery-powered surgical saw. We don't get much opportunity to practice here, I am a bit rusty, so I have been going out in the woods to practice by cutting up dead animals."

"Then you've been hunting without a license."

"The animals were already dead."

"Bull. I suppose you can lead us to the places in the forest where these cut-up dead animals are?"

Haquapar was quiet for a long time. "I'm not answering any more questions until I get a lawyer."

It did not take long to search Dr. Haquapar's apartment. It was a sparsely furnished one-bedroom basement suite with few places to conceal things. Haquapar had sat silently throughout the search, looking down at the table. Wesson then asked for the keys to Haquapar's truck, which was parked out front. Haquapar sullenly pulled the keys off a rack by the door and handed them over. When Archbold and Simmons had gone outside, Wesson sent Haquapar into the bedroom so he could dress more appropriately. He emerged from the bedroom just as Archbold returned to the apartment.

"Sergeant," Archbold told Wesson, "we've found something I think you should see."

They all filed outside. Haquapar's truck had a canopy over the box. The tailgate hung open, and there in plain view, among other assorted items, were a stained poncho and a pair of rubber boots.

"Are these yours, Dr. Haquapar?" Wesson asked.

The doctor replied, "Ask my lawyer."

"Then I'll have to ask you to get into the car."

"Am I being arrested?"

"Not yet."

The doctor sat uncomfortably in the backseat of the cruiser while neighbors looked on and the policemen finished their inspection of the truck. They bagged the poncho and the boots for lab analysis. Then Wesson, Archbold, and Simmons got into the car, and they pulled away from the curb. A short time later, they stopped in front of the clinic where Dr. Haquapar and several other doctors had their offices.

The receptionist's mouth dropped open in surprise as Dr. Haquapar and the three policemen walked into the clinic.

"Could you tell me which is Dr. Haquapar's office?" Wesson asked the receptionist.

She hesitated and looked at the doctor, who nodded. "Down the hall," she said, "third door on your left."

"Is the door unlocked?"

"Yes."

"Thank you."

Archbold and Simmons moved down the corridor toward the office while Wesson guided Haquapar to a seat in the waiting room. Wesson smiled. Haquapar slouched back in his chair, staring at his shoes and avoiding eye contact with the patients.

About twenty minutes later, Archbold and Simmons filed back out. Archbold held up some sort of electronic saw in a plastic evidence bag. Wesson and Haquapar got to their feet and walked out of the clinic.

"Thank you," Wesson said over his shoulder, smiling at the receptionist.

"You're welcome," she returned in an uncertain voice.

Once the saw was stowed in the trunk, the four men got into the car as before. They drove without speaking and pulled up in front of Haquapar's apartment. Wesson got out and opened the back door.

Haquapar climbed slowly out. "So you're not arresting me?"

"What for?"

Haquapar struggled for words. "I mean, aren't you going to ask me questions . . . about the saw?"

"I thought you were refusing to answer questions."

"I am."

"Then there's no point, is there?" Wesson said. "But we might have some questions for you later. So if you want your lawyer, you'd best go ahead and call."

The policemen drove off, leaving Haquapar perplexed on the sidewalk.

"Mr. Smyth?"

"Yes."

"This is Sergeant Prestwyck down at RCMP headquarters."

"Yes. Did you find out anything?"

"I talked to Mark Driemer, the truck driver, and to Grant Parkinson. I also talked to Detective Harder of the Winnipeg police."

"What do you think?"

Prestwyck hesitated. "Mr. Smyth, it's like this. Harder did a thorough investigation. The way he figures it, Mr. Rempel is a very successful businessman. He owned his own trucking company and then was vice president in a very successful firm. He must have been making pretty good money. So what did he do with it? Have you seen his house? It's no mansion, certainly not what he could have afforded. Harder thinks Rempel must have either been squirreling money away for years or had some expensive habits on the side. Harder had picked up hints that Rempel was doing some gambling and drinking that his wife didn't know about. And then you come to his wife. Look, Mr. Smyth, I know she is a friend of yours, but take a good look at her. She's older than her husband and . . . well, dowdy. Certainly Rempel could find a more exciting woman than that, with his money."

John Smyth opened his mouth to protest that assessment, then changed his mind. He could see that Prestwyck had a point. The only trouble was, he didn't know Jake Rempel.

"The way Harder figures it," Prestwyck was saying, "Rempel goes into work that last night, picks up the hundred thousand dollars he embezzled from the company—a final addition to the money he was squirreling away—and then finds a way to leave town without anybody knowing where he is going. Harder thought he had driven his car to the bus station and then taken a bus somewhere, or that was a ruse and he was picked up by a taxi or his new girlfriend in another car."

"But the new evidence?"

"It's really two months old, and it doesn't change anything. Maybe he did go to Prince George. But he still disappeared of his own free will, as far as we know. And he could have gone anywhere from there—bought a car or a plane ticket or a bus ticket or been picked up by someone else. The point is, he could be anywhere. He probably had a new identity already waiting for him that he established years ago. Could have another wife or mistress somewhere. He was a businessman, always going away on business trips, so he could easily have done that."

"Sergeant Prestwyck, I—"

"Mr. Parkinson says he isn't going to press charges for the embezzlement, by the way. That's not our preference, but he says the bad publicity would cost him more than the hundred thousand, and he's glad to be rid of Rempel. So there's no crime here, just a man leaving town for a new life. That's the way Harder figures it, and I agree with him. I'm sorry, Mr. Smyth."

Smyth sighed. "But how am I going to tell that to Elvira?"

"That's your problem." Prestwyck paused. "You could just tell her we're still investigating and we'll let her know if we find out anything. That's what we tell people all the—"

He stopped. "I'm sorry, Mr. Smyth. Good-bye."

"Thank you, Sergeant Prestwyck. It was good talking—"

But Sergeant Prestwyck was no longer on the line.

"Shouldn't we have brought Haquapar in for questioning?" Archbold asked Wesson later in the afternoon. They were sitting in the private office.

"Maybe, but Haquapar's been through the drill before. We probably wouldn't have gotten anything out of him. It might be more effective to let him sweat for a while. Besides, what have we got on him really?"

"We've got a blood-stained poncho, boots, and a murder weapon."

"We've got a poncho and boots, whose stains might or might not be blood. We've got a battery-powered surgical saw, which it is perfectly logical for a doctor to have. And we've got

170

a reasonable explanation from Haquapar for why he was out along the highway."

"A reasonable explanation?"

"Okay, a bizarre explanation, but one that might still be true. Haquapar is a bizarre character."

"But since we didn't arrest him and he knows we are on to him, he could be destroying evidence right now."

"Yes, but we only had a search warrant to look for the saw and poncho, not to do a general search. If there really is human blood on the poncho or saw, if it turns out to be human blood, and if we can match the DNA of that blood to one or more of our victims, then we can bring in a forensics team and tear Haquapar apart. If we don't find DNA, we don't have a case anyway, and trying to talk him into confessing would be a waste of time. By the way, have you found out anything else about Hawkins?"

"I talked to the people down at Williams Lake again. The accident that killed the reporter is not suspicious at all. The guy Hawkins beat up was a logger named Jerry Obladewicz. As far as they know, he is still in the Williams Lake area, but they haven't been able to track him down. They are still checking. I've also asked about the gang of kids who killed Hawkins's wife. They have all been released now, but three have been arrested on other charges."

"Could Hawkins have killed some of them and dumped their bodies up here?"

"Good question. I asked Williams Lake to check on them. They know where most of them are, but they are still trying to trace two of them. They aren't officially missing. They just don't know where they are. Besides, even now they'd be too young to be our bodies."

"Right. What about Luther Malone and Amber Long?"

"Still nothing. I don't get the impression that a murder

case in Prince Rupert, B.C., is a priority for the authorities in California, and Amber's—"

"Sergeant," Mildred interrupted, "we just got a nine-one-one call from some hikers about twenty-five kilometers out on the highway. They've been attacked by some guys with a chainsaw. Montgomery is out on patrol, so I've dispatched him and sent an ambulance."

"Come on, Archie. Get Simmons," Wesson said, jumping up. Rushing past Mildred's desk, he called over his shoulder, "If he's alone, tell Montgomery to approach with caution. Call anybody else available to get out there and back us up."

Flying up the highway with siren wailing, Wesson wondered what they would find. Was a chainsaw the murder weapon after all? How many would be dead this time? Would any witnesses be left alive?

The trip seemed to take forever. He could hear the ambulance siren in the distance behind them. At last Wesson, Archbold, and Simmons saw Montgomery's lights flashing in the small parking lot that served several hiking trails. Their car squealed to a stop beside his. There were four other cars in the parking lot. Three young women wrapped in blankets sat on the grass at the edge of the lot, an older couple hovering over them. Montgomery, who had been waiting beside them as well, approached Wesson as he got out of the car.

"What's the status?" shouted Wesson.

"No one's dead, no serious injuries, and the perpetrators are gone."

The adrenaline still pounding in their veins, Wesson, Archbold, and Simmons willed themselves to stand still. The ambulance squealed into the parking lot behind them.

"What happened?" Wesson barked at Montgomery.

"As far as I can understand, the three young women were

hiking a couple of kilometers in, went around a curve in the trail, and stumbled over a group of Native boys sniffing gasoline. The boys grabbed them and threatened them with knives. Then they started up a chainsaw and began cutting the women's hair with it."

"Man!" Simmons gasped. "That must have been terrifying."

"Are you sure there were just three women?" Wesson asked.

"That's what they say," Montgomery answered.

"How did they get away?"

"I'm not sure. The boys seem to have just gotten tired of the whole thing after a while and went back to their gasoline sniffing. At that point, the women beat it out of there and ran all the way back here. The older couple had just pulled in. They had a cell phone and called us."

Wesson looked over at the three young women, who were now being attended to by the ambulance crew. "Were they raped?" he asked in a low voice.

"I don't think so, although they were molested to some extent."

"They are probably in too much shock to be questioned thoroughly right now. How many boys were there?"

"Ten or twelve, one of them said. There would have to be enough to control all three women. The women aren't big, but they are hikers—athletic, you know—so they should probably have been able to put up some resistance."

"Did they recognize any of the boys?"

"I don't think so, but one of the women heard the name *Daniel.*"

"Archie, get on the radio. Tell Leblanc and the others to shut down the roadblock immediately and follow us to the Nootkasin Reserve. No sirens." To Montgomery he added, "You stay and finish up here. If any backup comes, send them on to the reserve. When you're done, you can come out too."

Wesson got back into the car, pulled out of the parking lot, and headed for the reserve.

"You figure it's Daniel Miniwac and his friends?" Archbold asked.

"Who else?"

"You think we have any chance of getting them without triggering an Indian—er, *Native* war?"

"The reserve's five kilometers from here. The women were running, and the boys apparently were not. If we could get to the reserve before the boys do and they are still all together, we might have a chance of grabbing all of them. Otherwise, we won't be able to tell who was with Daniel."

"Sure, but they've got to know they're in trouble. They might not even return to the reserve. It's more likely that they'll find somebody to hide them."

"It depends on how much gasoline they've been sniffing. They don't sound as if they're thinking straight. And to find somebody to hide them, they'd have to go back home. Some of the trails they were on come out on the road into the reserve. If we could catch them on the road before anyone on the reserve sees them or us, we might get lucky."

Wesson, Archbold, and Simmons got to the reserve before Leblanc and the others. They drove up the road almost to the village, turned around, and parked the car in the brush at the edge of the road, all the while hoping no one in the village had spotted them.

They sat there about twenty minutes and had just caught a flash of Leblanc's lights through the trees when two boys wandered out of the woods onto the road.

"Leblanc, kill your lights," Wesson barked into the radio, "and slow down. The boys are just coming out of the woods onto the road into the reserve. They're between you and us."

There were nine boys on the road now. They walked

slowly toward the village, staggering slightly from the effects of the gasoline. One of them carried a chainsaw on a harness over his shoulder. As Leblanc's car came up behind them, Wesson, Archbold, and Simmons got out of their car. Archbold was carrying a rifle.

"Whatever you do, Archie," Wesson whispered, "don't fire that gun."

The policemen were within ten feet before the boys even noticed their approach.

"Hello, Daniel," Wesson said. "You look tired. Why don't you sit down?"

Daniel stared stupidly at Wesson. Wesson noted that Leblanc, Johnson, and Rumple had gotten out of the other car and were approaching the boys from the rear. Wesson slowly squatted down. Daniel started to do likewise, lost his balance, and fell. A couple of the other boys sat down. One at the rear, catching sight of the officers behind him, turned to flee back into the forest. Moving more quickly, Leblanc made a grab and caught him by the jacket. Wesson could see two more police cars coming up the road.

With four cars and eight officers, Wesson made a quick decision. He motioned to Leblanc to put the boy he was holding into one of the cars. He spoke quietly to Simmons, "You and Rumple start putting the boys into the cars, one at a time. Do it calmly and quickly."

Archbold edged toward Wesson, still holding the rifle. "What do you think?" he asked quietly.

Wesson responded, "I don't know. Maybe it's the combination of gasoline sniffing and their long walk—maybe they're on something else too—but they seem to be in a passive state at the moment, and I want to get them into the cars before their mood changes. I also want to get them out of here before some of their relatives show up and this blows up into a confrontation. We've got eight officers here now, and that's all who are on duty. I want you to take charge of getting the boys back to Prince Rupert. Then read them their rights and get blood samples. I want to know what they are on. Be very careful with them because this is a very important investigation and I don't want it messed up. I don't want any bruises on them. Do you understand?"

Archbold nodded.

"One of the things we should do next is follow their path back through the woods in case there are more of them and they left someone behind. A proper search would require dog teams, but we don't have time for that. There are three or four hours till dark. By tomorrow, any other boys will have wandered off and any evidence might be contaminated."

"You mean that Bear Miniwac and the other *Natives* might have gone out and destroyed the evidence."

"Let's just say I want to guard against any such possibility." Wesson gestured to Leblanc to come over. "Pierre, I want you and Rumple to follow the boys' trail back to the hikers' parking lot. There might be others out there. Take rifles, a camera, and evidence bags in case you find anything. Be thorough, but by all means make sure you get to the parking lot before dark. Montgomery and I are going to go and talk to Bear Miniwac. If we get to the parking lot before you do, we'll start walking down the trail to meet you."

"You're taking Montgomery?" Archbold asked. "He's not very experienced."

"I know," Wesson said, "but we're spread pretty thin. I don't want to send Montgomery out in the woods with Pierre, either, and as it is there are only four of you to take in the nine boys."

"Okay, Boss. Just be careful."

The village seemed quiet, almost deserted, as Montgomery pulled the car to a stop in front of the band office.

"Stay in the car," Wesson ordered.

Wesson got out of the car, walked up onto the porch, and knocked on the door. A few moments later, Bear Miniwac himself came to the door.

"Bear, I need to talk to you for a moment," Wesson said. "We have just arrested Daniel and eight of his friends. They were harassing some hikers using a chainsaw. We caught them leaving the scene."

Bear's face was unreadable.

"I'm sorry, Bear," Wesson said. "The boys are high on something. We took them to Prince Rupert. We'll have medical tests done on them. You can come and see them tomorrow."

"How badly were the hikers hurt?" Bear asked through tight lips.

"They were more molested than injured. The boys apparently cut the hair off one woman with a chainsaw."

"They didn't kill anyone," Bear said pointedly.

"Not this time," Wesson said. "But fear is running pretty high right now."

"You're going to blame your chainsaw murders on the boys."

"Not if they didn't do them. We'll look at the evidence very carefully. But if they're guilty, I can't help that."

Bear was silent for several moments. "White people," he finally said. "You corrupt our young people with alcohol, gasoline, guns, and television, and then you arrest them for being corrupted."

"I won't argue with that, Bear, but what choice do I have? If they break the law—if they hurt people—I have to arrest them. The problem is, how do we uncorrupt your young people once they are corrupted?"

Bear said nothing more, just turned and shut the door.

An hour later, Wesson and Montgomery came upon Leblanc and Rumple in the clearing where the boys had assaulted the hikers. Leblanc and Rumple were photographing and collecting evidence from the scene. Leblanc straightened up.

"You didn't find any other boys?"

Leblanc shook his head. "The boys followed a trail. We found some spots where some might have branched off, but we weren't sure. We got here and started picking up what we could see. Mostly gasoline bags and cigarette butts. Some bits of cloth. A fair amount of hair blowing around. And those." Leblanc pointed to evidence bags containing two twenty-six-ounce whiskey bottles.

"No wonder the boys were so docile. It's amazing they were still able to walk." Wesson looked around. "We should have gotten a forensics team in here."

"We thought about that, but the wind's picking up. Hair and bags were blowing all over the place. Looks like rain coming in again. By the time you got a team in here, all the evidence would have been blown or washed away."

"I'm not arguing," Wesson said. "It was the right decision. I just hope this stands up in court. Lawyers and the media are going to be all over this case."

They arrived back in Prince Rupert just before dark and in heavy rain. In spite of this, the area in front of the police station was packed with cars and news vans. As the police car pulled up, reporters emptied out of the vehicles and converged on Wesson.

"Stand back!" he ordered. "I'll come out and talk with you in a few minutes."

Walking into the station and seeing Archbold sitting at a desk, he demanded, "Archie, what did you tell the reporters?"

"I didn't tell them anything, Boss."

Wesson looked dubious. "What's the situation?"

"The boys are in the holding cells. They slept most of the way back and are still pretty far gone. I got Dr. Kuhn in as you suggested, and he's checking them over and taking samples."

"We couldn't very well use Dr. Haquapar on this."

"No."

"What else?"

"Lynn is over at the hospital taking statements from the three hikers."

"Good."

"Did you find anything on the trail?"

"Gasoline bags, cigarette butts, hair, two whiskey bottles. We'll get it packaged up and fly it to Vancouver tomorrow. But first I need to get rid of the press."

Wesson went outside and stood under an umbrella while the cameras whirred. He announced, "We have arrested nine people in conjunction with an incident of harassment on a hiking trail. I want to stress that these arrests are in regard to the incident on the hiking trail and are not related to the murders that we are investigating. We will let you know more details tomorrow."

A voice called out from behind the spotlights, "Are you saying that there is definitely no link between this incident and the murders?"

Wesson hesitated, then tried to recover quickly. "I am saying that we have found no link between these suspects and the murders. These suspects have been arrested on a completely different matter."

Another voice called, "Sergeant, one of your officers was seen carrying a chainsaw into the police station. Did that belong to one of these nine people? Could it be the murder weapon?"

Wesson stared hard to see past the glaring lights. "A chainsaw was brought in, but only in connection with the harassment case. We do not know yet who it belongs to."

"Could it be the murder weapon?"

"I have no reason to think so."

"Sergeant, your officers were seen to be carrying plastic bags into the police station. Did those contain pieces of more bodies?"

Wesson was shocked. "No. The bags contained evidence. No more bodies have been found."

"Will more bodies be found?"

"I have no reason to think so."

"Sergeant, is it true that the suspects you have arrested are a Native gang?"

"We have not yet had time to interrogate the suspects. We have not yet determined their identities."

"But some of them are Native?"

"Some may be. I will let you know more tomorrow. Some may also be young offenders, so we might not be releasing their names."

Voices started to shout out further questions, but Wesson realized that he had already made a mess of the interview and that talking further would only make things worse. He shouted, "That's all! I'll let you know more tomorrow when we know more."

He turned to go into the police station and found a dark figure trying to come in after him. He turned, blocking the doorway, and stated emphatically, "Reporters are not allowed into the police station tonight."

"But I'm not a reporter," a cultivated voice replied.

"Oscar?"

"Good evening, Sergeant."

"Come on in," Wesson said resignedly.

The other officers looked up as the two came in. For the benefit of the newer officers, Wesson said, "Oscar Poole, legal counsel for the Nootkasin Native band." Turning to Poole, he said, "Your clients are still doped up. They are being examined by Dr. Kuhn at the moment. We probably won't even interrogate them until the morning."

"I would like to see them now anyway, Sergeant. Also, you should know that I will be advising them not to answer questions."

"Do you think we could at least get their names? Look, Oscar, we caught them in the act of assaulting three hikers with a chainsaw. I'm not out to hang more on them than they are guilty of, but if you tell them to clam up and don't help us get to the bottom of this, I'll just have to assume that this is not the first time for them and they've already killed six people."

Poole stared hard at the sergeant. "Let me talk to them now, and I'll see whether they might answer some questions tomorrow."

Wesson nodded.

Chapter 17

SATURDAY, JUNE 5

It was going to be a busy day. Wesson had gotten home about two o'clock for a little sleep but was back in the office by six thirty. Overnight, a forensics team from Prince George had arrived and collected clothes and other evidence from the boys and from the three victims, including scrapings from under their fingernails. The evidence bags from what the police were now calling the hiker incident had been flown out to the lab in Vancouver at first light. The evidence bags from Dr. Haquapar had been flown out the day before.

The interrogations began at eight, with one boy after another being taken from one overcrowded detention cell to the interrogation room and sent back to a different cell afterward. The interrogations were videotaped.

The first boy, a wiry teen of fifteen, slouched sullenly in a chair next to Oscar Poole.

"What is your name?" Wesson began.

After prompting from the lawyer, the boy gave it.

"Where do you live?"

"You know where I live—on the reserve."

"What did you do yesterday afternoon?"

"We went for a walk in the woods."

"Who is we?"

"He doesn't have to answer that," the lawyer said.

"Come on, Oscar, we know who he was with."

"Then why ask the question? You are asking the boys to incriminate each other."

"How many of you were there?"

The boy, gaining confidence, shrugged. "Don't know. Didn't count."

"Were you sniffing gasoline?"

The boy looked at the lawyer, who nodded. "Yeah," the boy said. "We do it all the time."

"Did you take any other drugs?"

The boy looked at the lawyer, who shook his head. The boy said nothing.

"Did you drink any alcohol?"

The lawyer nodded this time. The boy said, "Maybe."

"Did you see anybody else in the woods?"

"I am advising my client not to answer that," Poole said.

"And you are going to advise your client not to answer any other questions about assaulting the three hikers, the chainsaw, and whether they've done this before, right?" Wesson snapped.

Poole smiled. "My clients went for a walk in the woods. They are not going to answer questions about anything else."

The boy smirked.

And so it went. Poole allowed his clients to put on the record that they were all impaired and thus had diminished liability for anything they might be charged with. He did not allow them to say anything that might support any further charges. In the end, the boys were all charged with assault, and Poole agreed they could stay in detention until Monday, jail being perhaps the safest place for them.

It was still raining heavily, but the reporters remained huddled outside under a canvas canopy some of them had purchased from a local hardware store.

"At least this is doing some good for the local economy," Wesson mused, looking out at them.

Wesson also noticed something more ominous. Down the street, several pickup trucks were parked in a huddle in a vacant lot. Wesson thought he recognized some of the trucks and their occupants. Several had a history of arrests for various offenses involving alcohol, driving, and bar fights. He knew some nursed a strong hatred of Natives.

Wesson walked through the rain to the canopy. The reporters flocked toward him like ducks in a park toward an old man with bread. When everyone had settled into place, Wesson announced, "We have charged nine people with common assault. The victims were three young women who were on a hiking trail about twenty-five kilometers east of Prince Rupert yesterday afternoon. The young women were traumatized but were not seriously hurt. All were treated at the hospital and released. Those charged range in age from fifteen to seventeen, so we will not be releasing their names."

"Are they Natives?" Jason Thuringer demanded.

"The victims are not. As you know, we can't release any information that might identify young offenders."

"Are the young offenders suspects in the chainsaw murders?" Melanie Grayson wanted to know.

Wesson decided a lie would be the best way to defuse the situation. "No," he said. Turning away, he added, "No more questions."

Back in the station, Wesson met with his task force. "Okay,

we've gone over the reports. The dog teams have finished their search of other stops along the highway and found nothing, so we are probably only dealing with six murders. We still haven't identified who the victims or the murderers are. Any ideas?"

"I've compared the reconstructions with the photos of the missing persons," Leblanc said. "It's hard to tell with these computer drawings, but I didn't see any close resemblances."

Wesson nodded. "I didn't either."

After a pause, Archbold said, "I think the Native kids did it. We know they're trouble. They roam around in those woods, their reserve's only fifteen kilometers from the chain-up area, they had a chainsaw that nobody can explain why they had, and they're refusing to talk, which tells me they have something to hide. We already suspected Daniel Miniwac of stealing the truck from the hunters last fall. My guess is that the two hunters are among the second set of victims we found."

"But the most recent victims probably died more recently than that," Wesson argued.

"Yes, but they were very thin," Archbold responded. "Maybe they spent the winter barely surviving in the mountains and the boys killed them this spring. Or maybe the boys had them tied up somewhere ever since they stole the truck last fall, gave them very little food, and only killed them recently. Maybe Bear Miniwac kept them locked up so Daniel wouldn't get into trouble for stealing the truck."

"So he gets them off on the theft charge by implicating them in kidnapping, forcible confinement, and murder?" Wesson asked.

"Wouldn't be the first time something like that has happened. Criminals often commit bigger crimes to cover up lesser ones," Archbold said.

"That's just it," Johnson said. "Criminals usually escalate

their crimes. If these boys killed the other six people, why didn't they kill the three hikers?"

"According to the statements you took, the boys only grabbed two of the hikers, right?"

"Yes, the third backed off around a bend in the trail as soon as she saw the boys, and they either didn't see her or didn't care. The women were traumatized, of course, so their stories were somewhat incoherent and inconsistent. When I finally started sorting out fact from emotion, I got the impression that the boys didn't seem very interested in the women at first, just made a few lewd comments. One of the women told them to grow up or get lost—they used both expressions in their statements, but the original may have been a little more colorful. Anyway, that led to some more shouting. The boys approached the women and told them this was Native land and they should go back to the city. One of them tried a little groping and got his face slapped, and then the boys grabbed both women, and one of them picked up the chainsaw and threatened to, quote, cut up their bodies like the other ones, unquote. He held it near one woman's face and then tried to cut off her hair. But the chainsaw didn't cut hair that well—it got tangled up in the chain, some got pulled out by the roots, and they eventually had to cut the saw out with a knife. By that point, the boys seem to have lost interest in the game and gone back to their gasoline while the women ran back to their car."

"Listen to what they said," Archbold insisted. "'Cut up their bodies like the other ones.' I think they did all the murders."

"They watch TV like everybody else," Johnson responded. "It might be suggestive, but all it proves is that they knew about the murders, not necessarily that they committed them. And if they had committed the other murders, why would they stop this time?"

"Maybe they were more messed up this time," Archbold said. "And why did they have a chainsaw to begin with?"

"Maybe they were going to cut wood and build a fire. Maybe one of them happened to be carrying it when they decided to go for a walk. Maybe they didn't have a reason. Maybe they were so stoned that they took it because it was shiny and looked pretty."

The officers sat silently pondering the possibilities.

"Haquapar is also a possibility," Simmons finally said.

"Maybe," Archbold conceded. "I heard back from a couple of the places he used to live. There are some unsolved murder cases there—there always are—but none of the bodies were cut up like these victims."

"He could have changed his method," Wesson said. "In any case, the lab reports will give us a clear answer on him."

"He fits the profile of a killer," Leblanc suggested. "Loner, substance abuse, no close relationships, etcetera."

"So does Gerard Hawkins," Wesson said. "He lives in the area, he's skilled with a chainsaw, and he has a history of violence. He should still be considered a suspect." He paused. "The key may be the victims. If we could figure out who the victims are, then we would be a lot closer to knowing who the killer is."

Whenever John Smyth was away working on a weekend, he always found the next week very long. By Friday night, he was exhausted. Therefore, he slept in on Saturday morning. Then, for another hour, he and Ruby lay in bed, drinking iced tea and reading the newspaper. He carefully read the article on the four new victims of the chainsaw murderer in British Columbia, thinking that only days ago he had been driving down that same desolate highway. He looked hard at the reproductions of the victims' faces, thinking how awful it must have been for the victims and how awful it must still be for the victims' families.

The phone rang. Ruby answered, listened a moment, and then asked, "Who is calling, please?" She was very adept at protecting their home life by graciously telling business callers to phone John at work during office hours. This time she said, "Just a moment, please," and handed the phone over to John.

"Hello," he said.

"Hello, John, it's Elvira."

John winced. "Good morning, Elvira. How are you doing?"

"I'm all right. John, have you seen today's newspaper?"

"Yes, I'm looking at it now."

"Did you see the pictures of the people killed by the chainsaw murderer in British Columbia?"

"Yes."

There was a pause. Elvira took a deep breath. "John, one of the men looks like Jake, and the height and weight are right too."

"Yes, Elvira, I noticed the resemblance. But you have to remember that these computer drawings are not completely accurate. They miss details, and they end up looking like a lot of people. It very well might not be Jake."

"Yes, I know, John, but it might be too, and if it is . . . I want to know."

John sighed. "Okay, Elvira. What do you want me to do?"

"Could you contact your policeman friend and ask him to find out?"

"Yes, Elvira, I can do that for you. Are you going to be okay? Do you want us to come over?"

"No, John, you don't have to do that. Just find out, please."

"Okay, Elvira. I'll let you know."

After he hung up, Smyth looked at the pictures of the victims again. The big man could have been Jake, but if so, who were the others? The woman looked vaguely familiar in a general sort of way. The two thin men he didn't think he had seen before, but one never knew.

He turned to his wife. "Ruby, do you think this picture looks like Jake Rempel?"

"Let me see. Well, I suppose it could be. Who is it? Oh . . . one of that serial killer's victims? That would mean Jake is dead. How awful for Elvira."

John found the number in the phone book, dialed, and waited. He tried to make his voice sound secretive. "This is John Smyth. I want to talk with Sergeant Prestwyck." He had found that at times such as this it was an advantage to be named John Smyth. The police receptionist usually put him right through, thinking he might be an informer using an alias.

"Sergeant Prestwyck."

"Sergeant, this is John Smyth, the religious writer."

"Mr. Smyth, you're not going to try to make me change my mind about looking for Jake Rempel, are you?"

"No, Sergeant, it's not that. It's . . . well, you know the four new victims of the chainsaw murderer they found in B.C.? Their pictures were in the paper today, and both Elvira and I think one of them looks like Jake. Ruby thinks so too. The height and weight are right. And we do know he went to the Prince Rupert area. Look, I know you get a lot of calls like this, and we could be wrong, but could you please check it out?"

Prestwyck paused. "Is there a DNA sample for Mr. Rempel on file with the Winnipeg Police Department?"

"I think so. I think Elvira said they took his toothbrush and looked for hairs in the house."

"Okay, I'll have it checked out. I'll let you know." He paused. "Mr. Smyth, did you recognize any of the other victims?"

"Uh, not really. The woman looks vaguely familiar, but I don't really recognize her. Maybe she just reminds me of a movie star—someone I've seen a picture of somewhere."

Prestwyck paused again. "Mr. Smyth, you know this might mean that I was right? The woman might be the mistress or the other wife whom Mr. Rempel went to meet in Prince George. She is certainly younger and better looking than Mrs. Rempel."

This time it was John Smyth who paused. He finally said in a small voice, "I know, Sergeant, but it would still be better to know."

They came cautiously into the room like a group of bewildered refugees—a mother and her three children, one in her arms and the other two huddled around her skirt. Cautiously she approached Laura, the weekend receptionist, and held out a small card. "Could I . . . could I see Sergeant Wesson?" she asked.

"Mrs. Thompson," Wesson said from the doorway of the private office, "come in." The four of them shuffled as a group into the small room.

"Are you all right?" he asked.

"No," she answered.

"Well, I am glad you have come. Everything will be okay now."

"Mr. Hawkins broke into our house," she blurted out. "He is beating Gary."

For the first time since he had met her, Heather was wearing a short-sleeved blouse. Wesson noticed there were bruises on her arms. "Did Hawkins also assault you?"

She just stood and stared at him.

"Lynn!" Wesson called. When she appeared, he explained hurriedly, "This is Heather Thompson. Will you take a statement from her? And get her anything she needs." To Laura he said, "Get whoever is on patrol out to Gary and Heather Thompson's place. Have them approach with caution. Send an ambulance. Pierre, Rumple, come with me."

Once more, they were soon flying up the highway, lights flashing and siren wailing, this time through pouring rain.

Once more, getting there seemed to take forever. No one spoke, each officer absorbed in his own thoughts.

The gate on the driveway stood open, and a lone police car sat in the clearing. As they came to a stop, Constable Montgomery appeared in the doorway of the house and waited for them. They ran through the rain and ducked inside. The neatly kept house was now a shambles of overturned furniture and broken lamps. Gary Thompson sat on the floor, leaning against the couch. His face was a mass of cuts and bruises. One arm was bent at an impossible angle. A first-aid kit lay open on the floor.

Thompson's eyes were closed, and he seemed only semiconscious. Wesson turned to Montgomery. "Have you seen Hawkins?"

"No. When I got here, the place was as you see it. I called out, and no one answered. I searched the house, but there's no one else here."

Wesson pondered a moment. "Rumple, you stay here with Montgomery and wait for the ambulance, just in case Hawkins comes back. Pierre, you come with me."

They went outside. Wesson, squatting in the rain, thought he could see the faint outline of footprints leading back in the direction of Hawkins's place. "Let's take the car," he said.

They drove into the yard and cautiously emerged from the car. Wesson looked around the now-familiar scene. All of the sculptures were carefully covered with tarpaulins. There was a bang, which made them flinch and reach toward their guns. Hawkins had come out of the house and banged the door shut, and was testing the handle to make sure it was locked. He also had cuts and bruises, but he had washed and tended them and put on a clean lumberman's shirt. He walked toward the officers.

When he reached them, Wesson said, "Mr. Hawkins, I am arresting you on a charge of assault. Please put your hands up and lean against the car."

Hawkins slowly did as he was told. Leblanc checked him over carefully for concealed weapons. At one point he must have touched a tender spot, for Hawkins winced in pain.

Wesson read him his rights and asked if he understood them. Hawk nodded.

"Mr. Hawkins, did you just beat up Gary Thompson?"

"Yeah."

"Why?"

Hawkins shrugged.

"Was it because of Heather?"

Hawkins shrugged again.

"What is your relationship with Heather Thompson?"

"I've never talked with her. I just heard her screaming."

"When you were beating Gary?"

"Before. A wife is a precious gift, and she should be treated with love and respect."

"Are you suggesting Gary Thompson beat his wife?"

Hawkins shrugged again. "Ask her."

"We will. I've suspected he was beating her ever since I first met her, but I couldn't do anything until she asked for help."

"I could."

"We have to arrest you anyway, you know."

"I know."

"Why didn't you cut him up with a chainsaw?"

Hawkins smiled. "I thought about it."

"Did you cut up the others?"

Hawkins's face became serious. He said nothing more.

They had a long, quiet ride back to Prince Rupert. The ambulance carrying Gary Thompson had raced on ahead.

Montgomery and Rumple, after locking up the Thompson house, followed behind.

John Smyth's quiet Saturday was ruined. He felt deeply distressed—for Jake and Elvira Rempel, for the victims of the chainsaw murderer out in British Columbia, for all the sin, pain, and brokenness in the world. After lunch, he puttered around the house, fixed a couple of broken slats on the white picket fence in front of the house (the fractures courtesy of his rambunctious children), and finally went down to his basement office. The home Bible study group had not met the previous week because several of the regular participants had been away or had schedule conflicts, but they would meet the following Tuesday, and he needed to prepare the lesson. He got out a study guide and a Bible commentary, opened his Bible to the next section, James 5:1–6, and began to read.

He was distracted. His mind wandered. He had read the section over five times and still had not understood a word he had read. Then he finally got it. A few minutes later, he was on the phone.

"Sergeant Prestwyck."

"Sergeant, this is John Smyth."

"Again? Mr. Smyth, why do you keep calling me? It's a weekend. Why do you think I would even be here? Don't you think I have something better to do than come into the office on a Saturday afternoon?"

"Uh, well, you're there."

"What do you want?!"

Smyth hesitated. "Well, it's just that I think I know who the victims of the B.C. chainsaw murderer are . . . and I think I know who murdered them too."

Chapter 18

SUNDAY, JUNE 6

Sergeant Wesson did not go to church that Sunday. He explained to Sandy that he had too many things to do. Which was the truth. He and his task force had reports to read and to write, and he fully expected the process to take all day. The steady downpour outside kept the reporters in their hotel rooms, in their cars, or under their canopy and out of the way of the police. They had paid little attention to the arrest of Gerard Hawkins and had not learned of the investigation of Dr. Haquapar but instead had published stories with headlines such as "Native gang suspects in chainsaw murders." Fortunately, the local troublemakers who might be inflamed by such headlines also seemed to be waiting out the rain.

Inside the police station, the holding cells were full, with the nine Native boys in one and Gerard Hawkins in another. Hawkins had stopped talking altogether, not a huge shift for a man of few words. He did not deny beating Gary Thompson—

the evidence was incontrovertible, anyway—but he denied he had cut up anyone else. His chainsaws and other tools had been sent to Vancouver for analysis. Gary Thompson was still in the hospital, expected to recover. His arm had been set, but doctors were still concerned about his concussion. Under questioning, Heather Thompson reluctantly admitted that Gary was very controlling, that he had verbally abused her, that he had beaten her several times, and that he had been beating her when Gerard Hawkins intervened. However, she had not yet agreed to press charges. She also insisted that she had never talked to Gerard Hawkins, although she claimed that once or twice she had seen him at the edge of her clearing looking out from behind some trees. She had not told Gary about it for fear he would accuse her of being unfaithful and beat her again. She and the children were currently being cared for by social services.

About noon, so tired he was having trouble concentrating, Wesson called Len Archbold into his office to talk.

"So what do you think, Archie?"

"I think you're tired of reading reports and called me into your office just to help keep you awake . . . Boss."

Wesson smiled. "So keep me awake. What do you think?"

"I still think the boys did it. They are the only ones we know who have used a chainsaw on another human being. What do you think?"

"I think we are pretty well back where we started from. We have the same suspects, except that now most of them are locked up, and some of the other ones probably should be too. I also think that we won't get any answers till the lab starts reporting back on all the saws and such we've sent them for analysis. We're also still waiting for the detailed analysis of the first bodies. The lab in Vancouver is trying to determine exactly how long the bodies were frozen and how long they were lying out there in the bush. The last time I talked to them, they said they now think the bodies were only out in the bush a few weeks—maybe less—after they thawed out. They are also working at clarifying the type of saw used. Maybe they can even tell us what brand of chainsaw. They do amazing things in the lab nowadays." Wesson paused. "Now get out of here and stop interrupting me. I've got work to do."

"Right, Boss." Archbold smiled.

She was sitting primly on the conventional couch in her neat but ordinary living room. The afternoon sun shone on her silver hair. "Thank you for coming, Mr. Parkinson," she said.

"I was glad to come, Elvira. What can I do for you?"

"Did you see the pictures in yesterday's paper"—her throat caught for a moment—"of the four new victims of the B.C. chainsaw killer?"

"Yes."

"I think one of them is Jake."

"Oh, Elvira, I am sorry. I guess there is some similarity. Have you told this to the police?"

"Yes, they are checking on it now."

"I'm very sorry, Elvira. I know this must be very hard."

Elvira sighed. "Well, I think I've been convinced for some time that Jake must be dead and won't be coming back."

"Yes, I guess it helps to be prepared for the worst. Still . . . it's just terrible. Please let me know when you hear back from the police. In the meantime, if there is anything I can do . . ."

"Well, Mr. Parkinson, there is one thing."

"Yes?"

"Jake's salary. I would like you to continue paying it into our bank account as you have been doing."

"Well, Elvira, you know I have been doing that for the past couple of months, and I have been glad to do it. I can even continue it for another month or two until you get things sorted out. But if that really is Jake's body, then it just wouldn't be right to continue paying his salary. You don't have to worry about finances, Elvira. Jake had some life insurance with the company, and he had a good pension. With the survivor's benefits, you will have all the money you need to live on."

"All I need, maybe, but not necessarily all I would like to have," Elvira said primly.

"But, Elvira, I can't continue to pay the salary of an employee who is no longer working. The company cannot afford to pay it."

"The thing is, Mr. Grant, I don't think you can afford *not* to pay it."

"I'm sorry?"

"As I said, I think I've known in my heart for some time that Jake was not coming back. So last week, I started to pack up Jake's clothes and send them to Grace Mission. Before I did that, I checked all the pockets. Among other things, I found this note, in Jake's handwriting. It is just a question, really. It says, 'Did Grant and Mark cut up Peter and Charlene?'" She handed the paper over to Grant Parkinson, then continued, "I didn't realize what it meant at first, but when I recognized Jake's picture, it all fell into place. I think what the note means is this: Jake suspected that you and Mark killed Mark's wife, Charlene, and the dispatcher, Peter Taylor. They were the first two bodies found."

"But those people were killed in British Columbia."

"No, that is what you want people to believe. I think those people were killed in Winnipeg and cut up in your meat-packing plant, and then Mark dropped the bodies off beside the road on one of his trips to the coast."

"Elvira, I know you are upset about Jake, but it doesn't do

any good to make accusations like this. I assure you Mark and I have not killed anybody, let alone cut them up."

"I think you did. I also think that when Jake confronted you that night when he went into the plant, you killed him too, cut up his body, and dumped it beside the highway out in British Columbia." Her throat caught again.

"That's ridiculous, Elvira. Mark drove Jake to Prince George, and if he really was killed, he must have been killed by the serial killer out there."

"That's another thing. I don't believe Mark drove to B.C. that night. Remember the day or two after Jake disappeared? I was in and out of the office, phoning everybody I could think of, asking everybody if they had seen Jake. I'm sure that one of the people I asked was Mark. I can't remember now whether I phoned him from the office or saw him in the office —I don't remember things as well as I used to—but I'm sure if I keep thinking about it, I will remember exactly when I talked to him. Yesterday, I started wondering about it. I knew Jake always kept copies of schedules and things like that in his office at home, so I checked the schedule, and Mark wasn't scheduled to leave for a trip to B.C. that night."

"Elvira, I'm sure you are mistaken. Perhaps the schedule got changed. A number of our drivers were sick with flu about that time. I'm going to call Mark right now and ask him to come here and straighten this whole thing out." Parkinson stuffed the note into his pocket, pulled out a cell phone, and dialed. After a pause, he said, "Mark? This is Grant. I am at Elvira Rempel's house. Could you come down here? We need to straighten out some things. Do you know where she lives? Right. See you in a few minutes." Turning to Elvira, he said, "Mark will come down here, and we'll get to the bottom of this. I am sure that our records will show that Mark drove to British Columbia that night."

"Oh, I am sure they will. But if the police investigate thoroughly, will they find that the records have been tampered with? Will the government records at truck inspection stations between here and B.C. agree with your company records? Jake used to own a trucking company, remember? I know how easily records can be falsified."

"You are being ridiculous, Elvira. What are the odds that Mark and I would kill three people and just happen to dump their bodies in the same place that a serial killer in B.C. is dumping bodies?"

"Oh, I don't think there is a serial killer in B.C. at all. I think you and Mark dumped all the bodies there."

"This is getting sillier and sillier. Who do you think the other bodies are?"

"To begin with, I think the second woman looks somewhat like your wife, Shirley."

"Do you really think so? I know those computer drawings look like a lot of people, but do you really think that picture looks like Shirley? It's all just guesswork, you know. I heard the bodies were more or less beyond recognition. Besides, Shirley left me and has moved back to the States. And who else do you think I killed?"

"Well, that I don't really know. I can only guess. Jake told me that there were some homeless men who used to sneak into the yard and sleep at night. He didn't think you knew they did that, but Jake felt sorry for them, so he never had them kicked out. If I had to guess, my guess is that the last two bodies were the homeless men. And I would guess that you killed them because they saw you killing one of the other victims or disposing of their bodies."

"That is quite a story, Elvira, but purely fiction. Have you told any of your suspicions to the police—or to your friend John Smyth?"

"Of course not, Mr. Parkinson. I thought about it. But that won't bring Jake back, and it won't do me any good. You know, I really loved Jake, and when he disappeared, I was devastated. I had lived almost my whole life as his wife. But the more I thought about it, the more I realized how unsatisfying that has been—to live my life in someone else's shadow. Now he's gone, and I have nothing. I don't have a lot of my life left, but I don't want to spend it wasting away in this boring, comfortable home. I want to travel, see the world, buy nice things. If I told the police, you wouldn't keep paying Jake's salary, and then I wouldn't have any of those things."

Grant Parkinson leaned back in his chair. "Elvira, you really are very clever." He sighed. "Of course, Jake was always the problem. None of the others had close family or friends, but Jake—I always worried about Jake. I should never have brought him into the company. I should have just bought the trucking division and let him go."

"But Jake wouldn't have agreed to that," Elvira said. "He was concerned about what would happen to the workers."

"Yes, but that meant whenever I, um, instituted cost-cutting measures or made accounting adjustments, I had to keep Jake from finding out about it."

"But he did find out about it. He was worried that things weren't right. That was why he kept going into work extra hours. Is that why you killed him?"

Parkinson glanced at his watch and then out the window. He sighed. "Not really. It was that stupid design I used for the building, with the executive offices overlooking the plant floor. Maybe also the way I drove the staff to work harder and put in extra hours. Jake found out the same way I did, and I forgot to take safeguards even though I knew."

"I don't think I understand."

Parkinson glanced at his watch again and took a deep

breath. "I went into work late one night just after Christmas. I had gone into my office, but I hadn't turned on the light in my office yet. I looked out over the plant floor, and there was Mark cutting up two bodies."

"My word," Elvira gasped. That seemed to encourage Parkinson to tell the whole story.

"Apparently he'd gotten back late from a trip. As a driver, he wasn't supposed to have a key to the plant or know the alarm codes, but I'd given them to him because he came in sometimes to help me with certain projects I didn't want Jake to find out about. He saw a light in the dispatcher's office, looked in, and saw Charlene and Peter—well, having a good time. I don't know what she saw in Taylor. He was a bit of a nerd, never mentioned having any family, and no one else liked him. Anyway, Mark grabbed a meat hook, went in quietly, and drove it into their skulls. They never saw it coming."

"But wasn't there . . . blood?"

"Not as much as you'd think. Taylor had a mattress on the floor of his office so he could nap when he was there late waiting for a truck to come in. I think he even used to sleep there some nights. He had nothing to go home to anyway. They were on the mattress, so Mark just pulled the whole thing out onto the plant floor and started cutting up the bodies. That's when I saw him. I suppose I should have phoned the police right then, but I couldn't really believe what I was seeing, so I went down to have a closer look. I recognized Taylor, and I guessed what was left of the other body was Charlene. I walked up behind him and asked him what he was doing. He spun around and picked up the meat hook. He told me he had caught them in Taylor's office. I think he would have killed me too if I had raised any objections. But the thing was, I never liked Taylor anyway, and he was no great loss as a dispatcher. Charlene was a good-looking woman, but she was Mark's business, not mine. And Mark was useful to me."

Parkinson sighed, looked at his watch again, and then continued. "Who knows what Mark would have done with the bodies? Ground them up for hamburger meat, maybe. But I wasn't having any of that, not after all the effort I had put into quality control. So we cut up the bodies into manageable pieces, mangled the fingertips and faces so they would not be recognizable—I think Mark actually enjoyed that part—and packed them in the boxes we use for special gourmet products. We marked them as a special order for me and put them away in the freezer. Then we put the mattress and their clothes into the furnace. We cleaned and sterilized the saws and cleaned up the blood splatters in the dispatcher's office.

"The rest of it was easy. On the way home, Mark stopped at Taylor's apartment and cleaned out his personal effects. The next day he phoned the landlord pretending to be Taylor, gave his notice, and said the landlord could sell the furniture in lieu of giving two months' notice—there wasn't much there anyway. On his next trip, Mark used Taylor's credit card in a couple of busy stores where no one would remember him. Mark told everyone that Charlene had run off with Taylor, and I said Taylor had come by that night and quit his job.

"Mark moved a couple of months later, so the police won't be able to find any of Charlene's DNA at his place. She ran away from home at sixteen and hadn't talked to any of her family in the past five years. She won't be missed. And that's that. Even if you were to go to the police, they wouldn't believe you. There is no evidence to back up your allegations."

"What about the others? What about Shirley?"

Parkinson shook his head sadly. "Shirley was an only child, and her parents are dead. She originally had more money than I did, but over the years I gradually got all the assets transferred into my name. I told her it was for tax purposes, and she believed it. She was really quite naive sometimes. When we moved to Canada and bought Winnipack, I explained that due to Canadian law all assets had to be in my name. She never paid any attention to finances, anyway, as long as she had spending money."

His jaw tightened. "Then, three months ago, she suddenly announced she wanted a divorce. For the usual reasons—I didn't pay attention to her anymore; she didn't want to live in Winnipeg; she didn't feel fulfilled. And I couldn't let her divorce me. As long as we were married, I owned all the assets, but if we divorced, the divorce court might award her half. I realized that what worked for Mark could work for me. So one night I took her out to dinner late to 'talk about us,' then said I had to pick up something in the plant. I said it wasn't safe for her to stay out in the car alone, so she came in with me. Mark was waiting with the meat hook."

Elvira winced, and Grant Parkinson shook his head again.

"It would have been easy. The problem was that there were some homeless guys out by the loading dock, and they had seen us go in together. After Mark killed Shirley, I went out and found them and invited them in for some coffee and food. I had thought on the way in that there might have been three of them, but I could only find two. They came in, I led them toward the dispatcher's office, and Mark hit them from behind. The only difference was we now had three bodies to cut up instead of one."

"And Jake?" Elvira asked quietly.

"Well, Jake came into work and saw us cutting up the bodies the same way I saw Mark cutting up the first two. Only Jake turned on the light in his office, so we saw him immediately. Luckily for us, he decided to run downstairs instead of calling the police. We caught him at the foot of the stairs in the reception area and dragged him out to the plant floor. Mark killed him with the meat hook. Then he drove Jake's car down to the bus station, and I picked him up."

By now, Elvira was weeping softly. Parkinson's voice was almost tender as he spoke to her. "You see, Elvira, Jake really was the problem. None of the others would be missed, not really, but Jake would be. Even if their pictures turned up in the papers and somebody recognized them, chances are nobody would have cared enough to call the police and tell them. But Jake was different. Don't you see?"

She raised her head and looked at him through her tears. He looked away, glanced at his watch once more, and continued. "We couldn't keep the bodies hanging around forever, and Mark came up with the idea of taking them on one of his trips and dumping them in the woods. We waited until spring, when they would decompose more quickly and there would be more animals around to eat them. We assumed that might destroy the remains before anyone found them. Mark took the first two about a month ago and then the other four on his next trip. We didn't expect the bodies to be found so soon, if at all, but we had planned that if Jake's body was ever found, Mark would say he drove him to B.C. That way, the police would still be looking for his murderer in British Columbia— which is exactly what happened. We even changed the company records to say that Mark took a load out that night."

Parkinson glanced out the window again as a car pulled into the driveway. "There's Mark now," he said. "Don't get up. I'll let him in."

By the time the two men came into the living room, Elvira had pulled herself together. "So, Mr. Parkinson, I take it that you will be continuing to pay Jake's salary?" she asked.

"No, Elvira, I will not. I didn't get rich by paying money out needlessly. There is no evidence to back up your story, and

I don't think the police will believe you. They couldn't prove the case in court even if they did. However, I don't want to take that chance. So I think, Elvira, that you will be joining your husband."

Elvira gasped and put her hand to her face. Mark Driemer looked worried. "I don't think we can dump another body in the bush," he said. "People are going to be watching. I might get caught."

"No," Parkinson said. "I think Mrs. Rempel is going to be so disconsolate now that they have found her husband's body that she's going to commit suicide."

"I think not," Sergeant Prestwyck said quietly. Parkinson and Driemer whirled around. Prestwyck and two other officers had come into the room behind them, along with John Smyth.

Wesson and Archbold were still reading reports. "Archie, did you see this report?" Wesson asked. "Just before we called off the roadblock on Friday because of Daniel's gang, Rumple interviewed a trucker who had seen another trucker going into the bush. The second guy returned a few minutes later with an empty box. He said his refrigeration unit had gone on the fritz, and some of his load of meat products had gone bad, so he was just dumping it in the bush."

"That's disgusting," Archbold replied. "Illegal too. But it's unlikely to have anything to do with our case."

"I'm not so sure."

"Thank you, Mr. Smyth," Sergeant Prestwyck barked into the phone later that night. "You were right. I thought your theory was way off base. I'm still amazed that I let you talk me into that little charade."

"If you didn't believe in the theory, why did you let us go through with it?"

"Just to get you off my back, to tell the truth. I expected Mrs. Rempel would make the accusation and Mr. Parkinson would deny it and explain everything. Then maybe both of you would be convinced that he was innocent. Actually, it's a good thing I didn't believe you."

"Why?"

"Because if I had, I wouldn't have let Mrs. Rempel endanger herself like that. Mr. Parkinson could have pulled out a weapon and shot her before we could get in there from the other room."

"That was a risk she was willing to take."

"Maybe, but one I couldn't allow her to take if I thought the risk was real."

"Did you get Mr. Parkinson's confession on tape? Will it stand up in court?"

"Yes, we got it on tape, and I think it will stand up in court. It's a good thing too, because, other than the confession, we don't have a lot of direct evidence."

"I'll have to say the whole thing worked better than I had hoped. I was surprised that Mr. Parkinson revealed so many details of the murders. I hoped he would admit to the murders, but I didn't expect anything like that. Why do you suppose he said so much?"

"Because he had to fill in time while waiting for Mark Driemer. According to his confession, he got Mark to do all the killing. I don't think he has the nerve to kill anybody himself, so he had to keep Mrs. Rempel busy until Driemer could get there."

"Is that what he meant when he said Mark was useful to him?"

"Yes. I suspect that the night he saw Driemer cutting up

the first two bodies, he already had it in his mind that Driemer could kill his own wife. Otherwise, why protect a murderer? You don't do something like that just because you don't want to lose a good truck driver."

"Why would Driemer agree to kill Mrs. Parkinson and the others?"

"Because Parkinson could threaten to turn him in to the police if he didn't. And Parkinson had the means to reward him as well. In searching Parkinson's office, we also discovered that Parkinson was planning to promote Driemer to vice president of the transportation division."

"Jake's old job."

"Yes. Parkinson may not have promised that job ahead of time, but he probably promised some kind of promotion. You have to remember that Parkinson had been using Driemer before that for various schemes he didn't want Jake to find out about."

"That's right," Smyth mused. "I never thought of that."

"By the way," Prestwyck asked, "how did you figure out Parkinson and Driemer did it?"

"Well, one of the great things about being an editor is the information I receive. I get around a lot, and people send me news as well. It just happened that I was the only person who was in both Winnipeg and B.C., and I knew not only about the people missing from the meatpacking plant but also about the two missing homeless men. Jake had not told Elvira about the homeless men. I learned about that from another homeless man down at Grace Mission. Parkinson was right. There *were* three homeless men at the plant that night, but one of them got away. His name is Daft Darryl."

"Daft Darryl? I'm guessing he won't make a very convincing witness."

"Nor a very clear one. His mind is pretty scrambled."

There was a pause. "So it was luck?" Prestwyck said at last.

"Luck—or God's guidance."

"If you believe in that sort of thing."

Smyth smiled. "You know that I do. Anyway, there were two other things that helped put matters together in my mind. One was the Bible verse I was reading yesterday—James 5:6. It talks about rich men who have 'murdered innocent men.'"

"You're telling me the Bible prophesied these murders?"

"No. That verse was just describing what was happening in the first century. But human nature doesn't change. People do the same things today as people did two thousand years ago."

"Maybe. What was the other thing?"

"A sermon by Pastor Paul Postos in Prince Rupert last Sunday. He said that sometimes we don't see what is really there, only what we expect to see. He gave the example of someone saying the word *ball*. If you are on a beach, you might think 'beach ball' when in fact the person might be talking about a fancy dance. That's what was happening in this case. Because the bodies were found in British Columbia and because the most common high-speed saws out there are chainsaws, everyone assumed the victims had been killed there and cut up by chainsaws. That's why, as soon as they learned Jake's body had been found, Parkinson and Mark Driemer came up with that story about driving Jake to B.C. They had to keep the illusion going that there was a chainsaw serial killer loose in British Columbia. But once I connected more of the bodies to the meatpacking plant, I realized they probably weren't cut up by a chainsaw in B.C. at all but by meat saws here in Winnipeg."

Chapter 19

MONDAY, JUNE 7

Monday was a very busy day for Sergeant Wesson and his task force. Daniel Miniwac and his friends were released on bail. The lab in Vancouver reported that the charges of assault on the hikers could be substantiated. Traces of the victims' skin had been found in the scrapings from under the boys' fingernails. In turn, traces of the boys' skin were found under the women's fingernails. Clumps of one woman's hair had still been caught in the chainsaw, which was covered with the boys' fingerprints, but no human blood had been found on the chainsaw. There was thus direct evidence linking seven of the nine boys to the assault. The conditions of bail required that the boys be kept under close supervision by the Native band council and that they be forbidden access to alcohol or gasoline. The judge recommended that they get counseling, although there were no suggestions as to who might be able to give that counseling.

The blood on Dr. Haquapar's poncho and saw had been

found to be deer blood. Simmons and Rumple were out trying to find a carcass near the place where Wesson had seen Haquapar's truck parked, in the hope that they might find enough evidence to charge him with hunting out of season or cruelty to animals.

Gerard Hawkins was still in jail while authorities figured out how best to deal with the situation. The test results on his chainsaws had not yet come back from Vancouver, but the police were not expecting anything significant from that quarter. Gary Thompson had regained consciousness but was still in the hospital. Police were hoping to charge him with assault if they could convince Heather to press charges. Heather and the children were in the care of social services, which were urging them to find a safer place to live. Pierre Leblanc was trying to get in touch with Gracie Levasseur's parents to tell them that Gracie had definitely been in the area several months earlier and had apparently left in good health.

Sergeant Wesson spent much of the afternoon conferring with Sergeant Robert Prestwyck in Winnipeg. At four o'clock he sent Johnson outside to tell the increasingly impatient group of reporters that a news conference would be held at six o'clock. It seemed that Sergeant Prestwyck had an intense dislike of the media and wanted Wesson to make the announcement. It was also thought only fair to announce the arrests first to the journalists who had been following the case from the beginning.

By six o'clock, the reporters were fidgeting with anticipation. Wesson walked out of the station at five after six and crossed to the canopy area to address the bedraggled group. The skies were still dark with cloud, but the rain held off while Sergeant Wesson read from a prepared text that Grant Richard Parkinson, age fifty-one, a Winnipeg businessman, and Mark Alexander Driemer, age twenty-seven, also of Winnipeg, had been arrested in Winnipeg and charged with the murder of Jake Rempel, age sixty, one of the victims of the so-called chainsaw serial killer. The names of the other victims would be released in the near future, as soon as they had been positively identified, and further charges were expected. The case had been solved with the assistance of a tip received by the RCMP in Winnipeg. All of the victims were thought to be from the Winnipeg area.

Chapter 20

TUESDAY, JUNE 8

On Tuesday afternoon, Sergeant Wesson drove back up the highway and pulled into Gerard Hawkins's yard. He looked over at the tarpaulins that covered Hawkins's remarkable sculptures. The shrouded figures looked forsaken, like lost souls. *It was appropriate,* he thought. He had encountered so many lost souls scattered along this highway, both living and dead. And there were times when he had felt like one of them.

Leaving the sculptures behind, Wesson walked along the path toward Isaac's hut. The tarpaulin door was pulled down tight against the rain. When Wesson knocked and looked in, he saw Isaac sitting cross-legged on the bed at the far end of the hut. He seemed thinner and frailer than ever. His book, which Wesson now recognized as a Bible, was open on his knees. Wesson crawled in and sat down at the other end of the hut.

"Hello, Isaac," he said. "How are you?"

"Okay."

"We arrested Gerard Hawkins on Sunday. I was worried about you because Mr. Hawkins isn't around to take care of you now."

Isaac said nothing.

"He's the one who gave you the stove and the blankets, right?"

Isaac said nothing. Wesson waited. Isaac finally nodded slightly.

Wesson continued, "We arrested Hawkins for beating up Gary Thompson. Do you know anything about that?"

Isaac said nothing at first, then stated, "Hawk was afraid Gary was beating his wife. He thought he had heard screams sometimes, so he was keeping an eye on their place."

"Yes," Wesson said. "Anyway, Mr. Hawkins will probably be back home in a few days." He paused. "Abraham, don't you think it's time you went home too?"

The other man seemed to sag even more. "How did you know?"

"Just a guess. We've been looking for you for several months—had a pretty good description, though you've changed a lot."

The old man smiled ruefully and lifted a hand to his face. "The old nose still gave me away, huh?"

"Where is John Anderson?" asked Wesson.

The smile disappeared. "Things had been tough for us, John and me. That's why we became closer friends. We knew what the other was going through. One day, John said, 'Let's go hunting.' We thought it would be good to get away, so we went. We were farther out the highway toward Prince George. We had been in the bush all morning and hadn't got close enough to anything to get a shot. That was just how things were going. We had stopped to rest and eat a bit. Then John said, 'I'm sorry, Abe.' I didn't know what he was talking about. He got up and walked a couple of hundred yards into the woods, and—boom."

"He shot himself?"

"I don't think he had planned it ahead of time. He just sort of gave up all of a sudden. We were pretty far out by then, and I couldn't drag him out, so I covered him up with rocks and walked back to the truck. But when I got there, the truck was gone. It was just one more thing. A while before I got there, I thought I had heard an engine start. I walked back down the logging road to the highway, but there was nothing in sight.

"We found the truck," said Rempel. "But we could never find you."

He nodded. "I knew I should report what happened, but then I thought maybe things would be better if I just went away permanently. I didn't want to take John's way out, but I thought maybe I could just sort of . . . well, disappear. I was standing there thinking that when Hawk drove by. He stopped and asked if I needed help. I didn't tell him about John—just told him I had been hunting and someone had stolen my truck. He said he was going toward Prince Rupert, not back to Prince George. I said that was fine, one direction was as good as another.

"It was dark long before we got to his place, so he suggested I stay the night with him and he'd take me into Prince Rupert the next morning to report my truck was stolen. I said it didn't matter; it was an old truck anyway, not worth getting back—whoever took it would soon find out it was more trouble than it was worth. In the morning, Hawk gave me breakfast and then started working on his sculptures. I decided one place in the bush was as good as another, so I walked out a ways from Hawk's place and started building this hut. I only had a small ax. A while later, Hawk came along and saw what I was doing. He never said a word, just went away. He came back a half hour later with a chainsaw and helped me build this place. He can do wonderful things with a chainsaw . . ."

Abraham Rempel stopped and looked up as though the words had worn him out. It was probably the most talking he had done in months.

"You aren't really crazy, are you?"

The old man sighed. "No, although there were times I thought I might go crazy sitting out here all alone. But in a way, it's been healing too. When you came that first day, I hadn't heard you coming. You caught me by surprise. I thought that if I acted like a crazy old hermit who had been living in the woods for years, you wouldn't figure out who I was. I didn't want to go back. I didn't have anything worth going back to."

"But you can't live here for long. You don't have much here either."

"I have a friend." Abe sighed again. "I guess I should show you where John is. I can do that."

"Yes, that would be good. By the way, why did you call yourself Isaac?"

"Because in the Bible, Isaac was the son of the Old Testament patriarch Abraham. I was Abraham, and I sort of started a new life out of my old one, so I took the name Isaac."

"So you're your own son?"

"If you want to look at it that way."

Chapter 21

SATURDAY, JUNE 12

Troy Wesson and Abe Rempel sat in the private office of Prince Rupert's police station. They were looking out the window at the street when a blue Honda rental car pulled up and a small man with wire-rimmed glasses, a bald head, and a red beard emerged.

Wesson went to the front door to greet him. "Good afternoon, Mr. Smyth."

He ushered Smyth into the small office. "Mr. Rempel, this is John Smyth from Winnipeg. He was a friend of your cousin Jake."

After some small talk, John Smyth said, "Abe, I don't know if you've heard, but Jake passed away a few months back. His wife, Elvira, asked me to come here and invite you to go live with her in Winnipeg. She has a big house all to herself, and there is a suite in the basement they fixed up a few years ago. One of their kids lived in it for a while."

Abe thought awhile. "Yes, I remember Elvira. She's a good

woman. But I think I need to go back to Vancouver to sort things out there. It shouldn't take long. I already lost my house and business, and I guess most of my stuff is gone by now. But I'd like to check on a few things, tell a few people what happened. And I'll have to report to the police, I guess."

Smyth answered, "We can go there before we go to Winnipeg."

As they were leaving, Troy Wesson said, "Mr. Smyth, I would like to thank you again for your help in solving the murders."

"I didn't do much, just consulted the Person who knows all the answers."

Wesson looked puzzled.

"I prayed to God, Sergeant. Pastor Paul and I told you we were going to pray that the case would be solved."

"And I told you the case would be solved by hard work," Wesson reflected ruefully.

"That's partly true. I was working at something when I discovered the answer. I think that's a good combination."

"What? You and me? Smyth and Wesson?"

"No. Prayer and hard work. God and human beings."

Acknowledgments

M y thanks to Dick and Robin Knox, who provided valuable local information about the Prince Rupert area;
line editor Anne Christian Buchanan, whose improvements
to style, plot, and characterization were remarkable; Moody
editors Michele Straubel, Amy Peterson, and Lori Wenzinger,
who have believed in and supported John Smyth from the
start; and my agent, Les Stobbe, whose wise advice and abili-
ty to open doors have made publication of this book possible.

A *John Smyth Mystery*

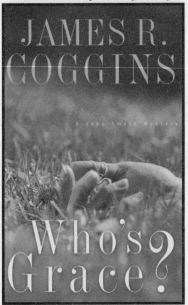

He stumbled past the vacant smiles of the flight attendants and down a narrow corridor in a long, turgid river of people. He turned a corner, passed through a glass door, and began descending some stairs. In the large, crowded room below him, people stood clustered around carousels waiting for their luggage.

At the far end of the room stood a policeman in a blue-and-tan uniform, one of the Royal Canadian Mounted Police officers regularly assigned to airport duty. Smyth hestiated, then slowly approached him. Without preamble, he stopped in front of the officer and stammered, "I think . . . I've just seen . . . a murder."

John Smyth witnesses what he believes is a murder as he is landing in Winnipeg, Canada. No one takes him seriously until a woman's body is found with a pendant bearing the name "Grace."

MOODY
PUBLISHERS

THE NAME YOU CAN TRUST®

Who's Grace?
ISBN: 0-8024-1764-7

SINCE 1894, Moody Publishers has been dedicated to equip and motivate people to advance the cause of Christ by publishing evangelical Christian literature and other media for all ages, around the world. Because we are a ministry of the Moody Bible Institute of Chicago, a portion of the proceeds from the sale of this book go to train the next generation of Christian leaders.

If we may serve you in any way in your spiritual journey toward understanding Christ and the Christian life, please contact us at www.moodypublishers.com.

"All Scripture is God-breathed and is useful for teaching, rebuking, correcting and training in righteousness, so that the man of God may be thoroughly equipped for every good work."
—2 TIMOTHY 3:16, 17

MOODY
PUBLISHERS

THE NAME YOU CAN TRUST®

Desolation Highway Team

Acquiring Editor
Andy McGuire

Copy Editor
Anne Buchanan

Back Cover Copy
Laura Pokrzywa

Cover Design
UDG DesignWorks, Inc.

Cover Photo
Getty Images

Interior Design
Ragont Design

Printing and Binding
Bethany Press International

*The typeface for the text of this book is
Fairfield LH*